HIS SOPHY

Clever. Stubborn. Exasperating. Adorable. His love and delight. And—memories of that other, earlier murder investigation revived—his despair.

Yet Lucian wouldn't want her changed. Not for all the ambassadorships in the British Empire.

He leaned forward and kissed the tip of her pert nose. "A penny for your thoughts."

She looked at him.

"You'd be paying for something you already know."

"I was afraid of that."

There was a moment of silence.

"You don't want to tell me why you were at Peter Marston's lodging house? Or is it that you *cannot* tell me?"

"If I believed for an instant that it would keep you out of the affair I'd be tempted to say yes."

"Lucian, don't tease. You know very well that, if it's not a state secret, I'll hear about it sooner or later."

"Even if it *were* a state secret," he said wryly.

"Well?" She started walking back toward the house. "What were you all doing in St. Martin's Lane? Did you find the missing dispatch in Peter's rooms after all?"

"No, Sophy." He easily caught up with her. "We found the place in shambles and Peter's old servant dead. Stabbed."

Also by Karla Hocker

The Impertinent Miss Bancroft

THE INCORRIGIBLE SOPHIA

Karla Hocker

ZEBRA BOOKS
Kensington Publishing Corp.
http://www.kensingtonbooks.com

ZEBRA BOOKS are published by

Kensington Publishing Corp.
850 Third Avenue
New York, NY 10022

All Kensington titles, imprints, and distributed lines are available at special quantity discounts for bulk purchases for sales promotion, premiums, fund raising, educational or institutional use.

Special book excerpts or customized printings can also be created to fit specific needs. For details, write or phone the office of the Kensington Special Sales Manager: Kensington Publishing Corp., 850 Third Avenue, New York, NY 10022. Attn. Special Sales Department. Phone: 1-800-221-2647.

Zebra and the Z logo Reg. U.S. Pat. & TM Off.

First Paperback Printing: November, 2002
10 9 8 7 6 5 4 3 2 1

Printed in the United States of America

To Mary Elizabeth
Thank you for letting me try my hand
at mystery and intrigue

One

Alert to the faintest of sounds in the dark street, he stood for a moment after the lodging house entrance shut behind him. Distantly, he heard the clock of St. James's Church in Piccadilly strike the hour of ten. He heard the rattle of carriages in St. James's Square to the south. But York Street itself was quiet.

His limp more awkward than ever, he started toward Jermyn Street. He must keep going. Livery stable first, to hire a fast hack for dawn. Then Dolwyn House. The dispatches were safe for now, but he must tell Barham.

He stopped and listened again. A chill touched the back of his neck. He had believed himself safe since he lost the pursuer earlier, somewhere between Whitehall and Bloomsbury. But, unmistakably, the footsteps were behind him again. A different set of steps. Quicker, lighter, more determined than the earlier ones. But with the same purpose.

It shouldn't surprise him. He knew they could not let him get away.

He did not look back but tried to walk faster. A futile attempt when every step was agony, when every step aggravated the hateful limp. He saw a light ahead, the lantern above the side gate of Brompton's Livery Stables. If he could reach it before the pursuer reached him, all might not be lost.

He was near the circle of light cast by the lantern. He saw the gate, the latch tantalizingly close. But the footsteps were almost upon him. He could hear the quick breaths of the pursuer—or, mayhap, they were his own.

He whirled, dropping into a half crouch, his fists balled. If he must die, he'd die fighting.

A little behind him, to his right, the gate creaked softly. His eyes remained fixed on the man facing him—the man who deftly twisted the silver top of his walking stick and unsheathed a long, narrow blade.

He could not make out the man's features, shaded by the chapeau-bras pulled low over the forehead, but he caught a gleam of light on curly blond hair showing beneath the hat and the glint of large gilded buttons on the man's driving coat.

Then the point of the blade flashed toward his heart, and all he could think was that, to the last, he was denied action. He had been prepared for a cudgel or a knife, weapons that would make his death look like the work of footpads. But he could not fight a naked sword.

He cursed the French, cursed Napoleon Bonaparte, cursed Madame Victoire . . . the bloody . . .

It was Wednesday, the third day of July, 1805. The Marquis and Marchioness of Dolwyn were holding a ball in honor of their daughter's eighteenth birthday. Lady Jane Hawthorne had made her curtsy to society this past spring. Her gentle manners, her sweetness of disposition won the hearts of the *ton*, and only two of the hundred and seventy-four invitations issued had been declined.

But even if Lady Jane were less than pleasing, the *ton* would still have flocked to the ball. The Season was officially closed, yet society lingered in town while across the Channel, at Boulogne, Napoleon amassed a fleet of invasion craft and an army, it was rumored, of 130,000 men.

London was the place to be during these unsettled times. Daily, couriers and agents arrived from the Continent to report at Whitehall . . . that the invasion force at Boulogne was incessantly practiced in embarking and disembarking . . . that Napoleon was waiting for Admiral Villeneuve to escort the invasion fleet . . . that Villeneuve was in the West Indies playing a cat-and-mouse game with Admiral Nelson . . . that Villeneuve had escaped Nelson, and the French ships were headed back across the Atlantic Ocean.

And while London, indeed, all of England, waited for the latest word from France, what better way to pass the time than at a *soirée* or a Venetian breakfast, at a rout or a ball.

In the gold, white, and royal blue splendor of the vast ballroom at Dolwyn House, Miss Sophia Bancroft turned laughing eyes on the tall hussar who had rescued her from a nerve-wracking catechism by the Dowager Duchess of Wigmore.

"Kit, you deserve a medal."

"Don't want a medal," said Lieutenant Lord Christopher Hawthorne, younger son of the Marquis and Marchioness of Dolwyn. "Give me another dance."

Kit was a good friend, and Sophy merely shook

her head, enjoying the bounce of her short curls. A few weeks ago, she had bowed to fashion and had her long hair cropped in the style first adopted by Parisian ladies who had survived the bloody revolution, a fashion which did not at all please the Dowager Duchess of Wigmore. But, then, nothing much pleased the old lady.

A frown creased Sophy's brow. "If her grace had asked me one more time why I continue to serve as governess to Lucian's niece and nephews when I am *supposedly*—you should have heard her tone, Kit!—*supposedly* betrothed to him, I swear I would have screamed."

"Would you?" Kit shot her a quizzical look. "In this squeeze? Without regard for Lucian's position?"

Sophy looked about her, at the throng of chattering ladies, the gentlemen engaged in serious discussion of the invasion threat.

Her mouth curled. Of course she would not have screamed. If there was one thing she did not take lightly or would in any way compromise, it was her betrothed's position as recently appointed aide to the Foreign Secretary, Lord Mulgrave. Lucian Payne, Viscount Northrop, a Whig within the Tory stronghold, was determined on a career in the diplomatic service. Whatever the provocation, she would bite off her tongue rather than impede his rise on the ladder to an ambassadorship.

"Listen, Sophy. They're striking up for the next set. Won't you reconsider?"

"We've danced twice, Kit. I don't mind being called eccentric because of my position in Lucian's household, but I shan't be called *fast.*"

He grinned. "Just testing, m'dear. Shall I fetch

you some punch? Or would you like to take a turn on the terrace?"

"A breath of air would be lovely."

Resting one gloved hand on the blue cloth of his tunic sleeve, she walked with him past the dance floor toward the open French doors leading onto a terrace and thence into the strip of greenery which, in town, was proudly called a garden. Not all town houses boasted a garden; Dolwyn House did and so did Lucian's house in Clarges Street.

One peek at the lantern-lit terrace, however, made them turn back. The crush there was thicker than the crowd in the ballroom.

"Couldn't take a step without treading on someone's toes," grumbled Kit.

"Never mind. Let's go into the salon. Perhaps Lucian has arrived."

They went into the foyer, deserted by all but the footmen stationed at the open front door. It was cool here compared to the stifling, perfumed atmosphere in the ballroom. The lively dance tune rendered by two energetic string quartets and the incessant ebb and swell of hundreds of voices were comfortably muted.

"This is as pleasant as a stroll in the garden," said Sophy, slowing her steps as they approached the salon to the right of the front door.

And then she stopped walking altogether. Three gentlemen entered the house: Mr. Pitt, the Prime Minister; Lord Mulgrave, the Foreign Secretary—and Lucian. Her betrothed.

She had entered his employ in mid-January, governess to his niece and nephews while their parents were in China. Before the end of the month he had asked her to marry him. Now, after five months, the mere sight of him still made her pulse quicken.

He was handsome, of course, and as dark as his brother, the Honorable Andrew Payne, was fair. But so was Kit Hawthorne dark and handsome. And Kit was certainly the more dashing in his regimentals of the Fifteenth King's Light Dragoons, the hussars.

No, it was really quite inexplicable that she had fallen in love with Lucian. He was stubborn—at least as stubborn as she was. He could be toplofty. And his notion of responsibility clashed all too often with her own. Yet none of this mattered when he looked at her, when his mouth softened in a smile for her, a smile that kindled a gleam in his green eyes.

His eyes were on her now as he left his companions and strode toward her. Tactfully, Kit moved away to play host to the Prime Minister and the Foreign Secretary.

"Sophy." Lucian's voice was a caress.

Her face glowed. "I was beginning to fear I wouldn't see you at all this evening. It must be past midnight."

"Barely eleven-thirty."

He caught her hand, turned it over, and pressed a kiss onto her wrist. The thin silk of her glove was no barrier to his touch, his warmth. She wanted to wind an arm around his neck and kiss him thoroughly, but the future wife of a future ambassador must show decorum.

She pressed his hand before releasing it. "In that case we'll have time for a couple of dances before supper."

"My love, I am sorry." He gave her a rueful look. "Duty still calls."

"Another emergency meeting?" She glanced at Mr. Pitt and Lord Mulgrave, who bowed politely, then moved purposefully toward the stairs. "At Lady Jane's birthday ball?"

"I'm afraid so. As I understand it, Castlereagh, Barham, and Sir Jermyn Leister are already closeted with Lord Dolwyn."

"Sir Jermyn—in that case it'll be a lengthy session."

Lucian Payne did not miss the shadow of disappointment crossing his betrothed's face, the frown that briefly darkened the clear eyes. Most often Sophy's eyes were a translucent gray, but this evening they reflected the blue of her gown.

They were eyes that had fascinated him from the moment of her arrival at Payne House, at night, during the height of confusion when a guest's missing diamond necklace had been found in his Aunt Addie's shawl. Sophy's eyes fascinated him still, held him captive with their clear, steady gaze.

He bent and kissed her cheek. "I'll do my best to keep the meeting brief. Save me a dance, will you?"

"Of course," she said warmly.

Kit rejoined them. "Lucian, old boy, I've been trying to act your deputy. But Sophy says she cannot grant me more than two dances."

"Be grateful." Lucian clapped his friend on the shoulder. "She saved you from having your cork drawn."

Almost a head taller, Kit grinned at Lucian. "Did she now?" he drawled. "If you weren't required upstairs, I'd suggest we try our paces."

Chuckling, Lucian turned away. "Then I'm glad I *am* required."

Sophy watched him mount the stairs. Lord Dolwyn's study was on the first floor, and on the night of his daughter's birthday ball the marquis was hosting a Whitehall meeting.

"Something serious is going on," she murmured.

"Something nefarious," Kit said grimly. "Treason."

She shivered. The July night was warm, and treason was no new subject at Whitehall. But with the threat of invasion hanging over their heads, the word held a doubly sinister ring.

Glancing into the crowded salon, she said, "Please take me outside, Kit."

He raised a brow. "Out into the square?"

She nodded. Walking in Berkeley Square at night might not be *comme il faut*, but nobody could be proper all the time. And Kit might be asked for information about this meeting, but he would never mention it in front of others. "I don't want to be squeezed to death on the terrace."

With a bow, Kit proffered his arm and ushered her down the red-carpeted front steps, brightly lit by flambeaux affixed to the front of the house.

For hours, the square had rung with the rattle of wheels, the clatter of hooves, as carriage after carriage drove up to disgorge jeweled ladies in diaphanous gowns and gentlemen in silk knee breeches and fancy dress coats at the canopied entrance. Now, the carriages stood still, lined up around the central garden and along Berkeley Street and Charles Street. The only sounds were the coachmen's rumbling voices, the strains of a lively country dance mingled with the talk and laughter that spilled through the open windows of Dolwyn House.

Festive sounds, soothing, blunting the ugliness of treason.

"What else can you tell me about tonight's meeting?" Sophy asked.

"Nothing, I'm afraid," said Kit. "You know I'd tell you if I knew anything."

Sophy nodded as they turned right, toward the south end of Berkeley Square, and walked slowly past the stopped carriages. Kit was unusually quiet, but Sophy did not mind, amusing herself by listening to the coachmen and grooms gossip about their masters and mistresses.

The tone of the servants' voices changed as they went along. Ahead of them, well outside the light cast by the flambeaux, several coachmen were heatedly discussing pamphlets that had littered the London streets a week earlier. Pamphlets from across the Channel. Proclamations from the Emperor Napoleon, promising rank and riches to the English populace if they allowed the French fleet to land unimpeded and assisted in the overthrow of King George and his government.

"It's all lies!" one of the men shouted.

Kit, apparently listening as well, muttered, "Of course it's lies, you fools."

"But what if it's true?" This was a young voice, thin and reedy, and very belligerent. Sophy recognized it as the voice of the Dowager Duchess of Wigmore's coachman and marveled again at the incongruity of that piping sound coming from someone with the powerful frame and bold stance of a prize fighter. "What if there is rewards, eh? Instead o' drivin' the old lady, I could set up with me own coachin' inn."

"Or, mayhap, you'd be made a dook!"

Tugging on Kit's sleeve, Sophy stopped. The sarcastic remark had come from Samuel Trueblood,

Lucian's trusted old coachman, who had driven her and Lucian's aunt to the ball. Her eyes had adjusted to the dark, and judging by the younger man's stance and balled fists, Samuel might be in a spot of trouble.

But if he was aware of the other man's anger, Samuel Trueblood gave no sign of being intimidated.

"Listen, Will, my lad," he said. "Lord Northrop saw pamphlets like that last year already. Showed 'em to us at Payne House, he did. He said that French upstart will no more help the English workin' man than he does the French. And if you had a smidgen of brain in your cockloft, you'd know that's so."

"Aye," said an oldster. "He's a great one fer lookin' after his own, is Bonaparte. If he has ter have dooks, he'll pick 'em among his brothers."

"Besides—" Samuel stabbed a finger at the younger man's chest. "D'you want a French emperor lordin' it over you as King of England? Made hisself King of Italy, didn't he?"

"Hear, hear," Kit said approvingly. "I wish Mr. Fox had your good sense."

Snatching off their hats, most of the men swung around to stare at Kit and Sophy. But Samuel, except for a quick glance over his shoulder, paid no heed to the interruption. He hadn't fired his heaviest gun yet.

"And what d'you think he'd do to our king, Will Ellison?" he demanded of the dowager duchess's young coachman. "Chop his head off, that's what."

Silence followed his words. The people might grumble about the state of affairs in England, but no one wanted to see the king beheaded. They liked gruff old Farmer George, be he sick or hale.

Somewhere, a clock struck midnight.

Slowly, Samuel Trueblood turned. "Miss Sophy, the streets ain't no place for a young lady. Does Miss Addie know you're traipsin' around out here? Or his lordship?"

"No one knows." Sophy cocked her head. "And no one will—unless you're going to tell?"

Lucian's coachman smiled grimly. "Only if I'm asked, Miss Sophy."

"Thank you, Samuel." With a sigh, she looked at Kit. "I am ready to return to the ball."

Samuel Trueblood pulled a length of tobacco from a pocket. He bit off a chunk. Chewing, he watched his master's betrothed and Lieutenant Lord Christopher Hawthorne until they disappeared inside Dolwyn House.

A lone carriage rattled into the square from Berkeley Street. A barouche, with its top down.

"Now, that's a late one," said the coachman of the Honorable and Mrs. Cyril Piercepoint, a couple notorious for arriving first and leaving last at any function.

Samuel cast a look at the barouche's lone occupant, dimly visible in the light of the lantern dangling from a hook on the driver's seat. A female in a cloak such as ladies wore when driving on dusty country lanes. A female in a wide-brimmed, veiled hat.

"If she's goin' to the ball," he said, "I'll swallow me whip. You ever seen a lady go to a ball in a hat and veil? And without an escort? And in an *open* carriage?"

The barouche stopped at the corner of Charles Street, two stately buildings south of Dolwyn House.

The coachman who drove Sir Jermyn Leister, a member of the Board of Admiralty, offered, "It's one o' them bits o' muslin, no doubt. Come to meet her lover."

The suggestion was received with sniggers and questions like "What'll she do, then? Send in her card on a silver tray an' ask Lord So-an'-so ter step outside?"

Sir Jermyn's coachman drew himself up. "Seen it more than once. The gentleman sends a note to the bit o' muslin ahead o' time, then leaves the wife at the ball and goes off to have hisself a bit o' fun."

"I daresay you know," piped Will Ellison, recovering from the set-down he had received earlier. "Ain't it what Sir Jermyn does?"

Sniggers again, but the men lost interest in Sir Jermyn's opera dancers and West End comets when the barouche started to roll again.

As soon as the vehicle turned the corner into Charles Street, they saw the gentleman standing at the curb. A minute earlier he hadn't been there. Or, mayhap, he had stood there all along, hidden from view by the carriage.

He crossed Charles Street and started toward Dolwyn House. Something about his step and posture suggested youth and vigor, an impression confirmed when he entered the circle of light cast by the flambeaux. There was no mistaking the broad shoulders and slim waist beneath the well-cut coat, the muscular calves in pale silk stockings. He wore his chapeau-bras at a jaunty angle and twirled a silver-topped walking stick. Indeed, it was a very smartly turned out young gentleman who sauntered up the red-carpeted steps of Dolwyn House.

"Samuel," said the Piercepoint coachman, "ain't he your master's brother? The Hon'rable Andrew Payne?"

Before Samuel could answer, a second gentleman rounded the corner of Charles Street. He, too, wore his chapeau-bras at a rakish angle and carried a silver-topped walking stick. He, too, displayed a fine set of shoulders and a shapely leg as he approached Dolwyn House.

Samuel Trueblood directed a stream of tobacco juice at a spot in the street where a cobblestone was missing.

"Could've sworn the first one was Andrew Payne," he said, his eyes on the second gentleman. "But look at this one. Walks like Master Andrew. Carries his shoulders like Master Andrew. Would have to see the hair to know which one is him."

"It's as they says," muttered the coachman in the employ of Lord Castlereagh, the Secretary for War. "At night all cats are gray. And one young blade looks much like another."

Two

In the foyer of Dolwyn House, the first gentleman handed his hat and walking stick to a footman, then stopped in front of a large gilt-framed mirror hung between gold-leaf wall sconces. A tug on the froth of lace at throat and wrist, a touch of long, slim fingers to hair the same rich, glossy hue as the mahogany table beneath the mirror, and he was ready to make an entrance in the ballroom.

He had taken only two or three steps when a footman murmured a greeting to yet another latecomer. An urgent demand to be told where Lord Barham and Sir Jermyn Leister might be found made the first gentleman turn around.

"Andrew, *mon ami!*" he exclaimed. "Well met. I was hoping I need not face Véronique alone. She can be quite a little shrew, my pretty *cousine,* when she believes herself slighted. But your presence," he added, his French accent becoming more pronounced the longer he spoke, "will save me from the raking over the coals for my tardiness."

Tossing hat and walking stick to the waiting footman, Andrew Payne strode toward the young Frenchman. As he passed beneath the chandelier, Andrew's hair gleamed like newly minted gold coin.

"Sorry, Louis. I fear I'm in disgrace, too. Your

cousin was kind enough to promise me two dances, but now—" Andrew raked a hand through his hair, a gesture that did nothing to smooth the unruly blond locks. "The devil of it is, I must pass some news to Lord Barham. Most likely that'll take him hotfoot to the Admiralty—with me in tow."

"Trouble?" Louis de Bouvier's voice and look conveyed concern.

Andrew shrugged. "There's always trouble," he said lightly. "Will you make my apologies to Mademoiselle Véronique?"

"I shall do better than that. While you speak to Lord Barham, I will find Véronique and bring her out here. That way, she will see for herself it is the powerful First Lord of Admiralty who prevents you from keeping your promise."

"Thank you, Louis. You're a true friend."

After a refreshing glass of champagne, Kit helped Sophy look for Miss Adelaide Payne, Miss Addie to all and sundry. She was Lucian's aunt, Sophy's chaperone. Having searched the ballroom in vain, he finally spied the lady's silver-gray head in the crowded salon.

On the sofa beside Miss Addie sat Lady Jane Hawthorne, Kit's sister, in whose honor the ball was held.

Miss Addie's still smooth, rose-complected face broke into a smile when she saw Sophy and her escort approaching. She waved, and so did the ostrich plume in the silvery hair.

"Kit, dear boy! You're just in time to take your sister back into the ballroom. I've been telling her she mustn't waste another moment chatting to an old woman. This is *her* ball. She must dance until her slippers wear out."

"Indeed, she must," said Kit. He held out a hand. "Come along, Janey. Let's find you a partner before Mama notices you're not on the dance floor."

A tinge of color stole into Lady Jane's heart-shaped face. Her eyes, wide set and dark gray like Kit's, briefly met Sophy's eyes before settling on her brother.

"Very well," Jane said quietly and rose, a slender girl with hair the color of dark honey. She carried herself with dignity and poise despite her tender years.

Taking the seat vacated by Jane, Sophy watched brother and sister depart and wondered why no one but she understood that Lady Jane preferred Miss Addie's company to that of any dancing partner as long as Andrew Payne had not made an appearance. Andrew, Miss Addie's younger nephew, was bound to look for his favorite aunt before he ventured into the ballroom, and Sophy felt certain there was at least one dance kept open on the gilt-edged program dangling from Lady Jane's wrist.

"What about you, Sophy dear?" said Miss Addie. "Shall I find a partner for you?"

Sophy wanted only one partner.

She was spared a reply, for in the same breath Miss Addie continued, "I needn't bother, I see. There's Lucian. And that charming Monsieur de Bouvier. And Andrew, too. What a naughty boy he is, arriving so late! But one thing is certain. You'll not lack a dancing partner now."

Sophy turned her head quickly. Her gaze flew to the door opening from the foyer. Her mouth curved in a smile.

Lucian. Slim, not as tall as his companions, he yet caught her attention to the exclusion of anyone else.

He crossed the room with his long, impatient stride, skillfully sidestepping clusters of gossiping matrons and footmen carrying trays of champagne.

"Sophy, love. I am very sorry, but Andrew and I must leave."

Swallowing disappointment, she glanced at Andrew and Louis de Bouvier, who were accompanied by Louis's cousin Véronique. She could only be glad that Jane had left with Kit. Andrew's infatuation with the beautiful Frenchwoman was no secret.

Offering her seat beside Miss Addie to Véronique de Bouvier, Sophy stepped close to Lucian.

"Something is the matter. What happened, Lucian?"

"Trouble."

He brushed the tip of a finger against her cheek. "Believe me, this is not what I envisioned for us when I sent Nurse Appleby and the children into the country. I wanted to be at your side when you made your entry into society. I wanted to dance with you, present you to my friends."

She wanted his company, too. More than anything. But she said, "I have your aunt. Don't worry about me. Miss Addie is doing everything for me that you'd do."

She cocked her head. The look she gave him was mischievous but also a little sad. "Except dance with me."

He hated having to deny her—and himself—that simple pleasure. He wanted to forget the trouble at Whitehall for a few minutes, wanted to be drawn into the magic spell of the music, to step in perfect unison with Sophy. He wanted to hold her hand in his and, when they reunited after a dance movement separated them, to kiss her forehead, her soft cheek.

He raised her hand to his lips. "Do you know, Sophy, there are times when I regret having accepted the post at the Foreign Office."

"No! Don't say that!" She spoke sharply, guiltily. "Or you'll make me regret having accepted your offer."

"I hope not." He did not want to part on a serious note and allowed a light, bantering tone to creep into his voice. "It was hard enough the first time to convince you to marry me. I don't want to have to persuade you again."

Andrew tapped him on the shoulder. "We had better go, old boy. You were granted a minute to bid your betrothed a good night. I'm afraid you've already trebled that time."

Lucian's eyes held Sophy's. "I love you."

He turned and walked off with his brother.

Sophy stood beside Miss Addie and the de Bouvier cousins amidst the laughing, chattering throng of elegantly gowned ladies and gentlemen.

I love you, too, Lucian. And I want an opportunity to tell you so.

In the doorway, Andrew looked over his shoulder. He raised a hand and impudently blew a farewell kiss toward . . . Miss Addie? The elderly lady certainly acknowledged the gesture, but Sophy was willing to bet the kiss was meant for Véronique de Bouvier.

"I wonder what has happened?" said Mademoiselle de Bouvier in her soft, musical voice that held just a trace of a French accent. "I heard that Mr. Pitt was here, and Lord Castlereagh. But they left, quite upset about something. And now, Mr. Payne told me, he and Lord Northrop must rush off to Whitehall."

"Another secret document missing at the Admiralty, no doubt. Or at the War Office," Louis de Bouvier said curtly. His English was as fluent as Véronique's, but the accent was heavier.

Sophy turned to him. "You sound angry, monsieur. Do you know more about the situation than we do?"

"I know what everyone knows. That there is a traitor at the Admiralty who passes information to Bonaparte's agents."

"Indeed," said Véronique. "More than once have I heard the word 'traitor' whispered this evening. But there is no proof." She looked straight at Sophy. "Is there, Miss Bancroft?"

Sophy recalled Andrew's words when he and Lucian were speculating about the papers that were either "lost" or "mislaid" at the Admiralty and the Horse Guards. He had said that proof was catching the miscreant with the document in his hand. But whatever Lucian and Andrew discussed in the privacy of their home was no one's business.

She shrugged lightly, dismissively. "I know no more than anyone else does—that occasionally documents are feared missing but eventually turn up again."

"And I wager, Miss Bancroft," said Louis, "that while those papers were missing, they were copied." A dark look crossed his face. "If something is not done immediately, we, the *émigré* families, will yet have to bow to the Jacobin rabble."

"Surely not." Miss Addie patted his arm in a motherly fashion. "My dear Monsieur de Bouvier, if you're afraid the invasion may succeed, let me remind you that Napoleon Bonaparte and his followers are not Jacobins. France is now an imperial state, not a republic."

Véronique smiled at her cousin. "Louis, *mon cher.* You must not spread your pessimism among our kind English hosts. Perhaps it is fortunate after all that you must be out of town for a little while. When you return, I daresay you will be in much better spirits."

"There's no fear of pessimism spreading in England." Miss Addie spoke without heat but with the conviction of an Englishwoman born and bred. "No matter how much bungling may occur at the Admiralty, we still have our dear Lord Nelson to stop any fleet Napoleon plans to send across the Channel."

"Dear ma'am, you are absolutely correct," said Louis, brightening. "I am a fool to have allowed myself to be plagued by concern. But thanks to your timely reminder I shall be able to leave town with a quiet mind."

He bowed with exquisite grace, his smile including Miss Addie and Sophy as well as his cousin. *"Au revoir, madame. Mesdemoiselles."*

As he was about to walk off, he said over his shoulder, "Véronique, you will not forget to make my excuses to Lord and Lady Dolwyn? And to give my messages to Lieutenant Marston and to Mr. Payne?"

"I will forget nothing. *Au 'voir,* Louis."

A frown knitted Sophy's brow as she watched Louis de Bouvier's retreating back. She did not question the message for Peter Marston, the young naval lieutenant with the ready smile and the awkward limp. Peter Marston usually sought her out for a companionable chat. This evening, however, she had not seen him at all. She assumed he was working late at the Admiralty.

But a message for Andrew? Louis de Bouvier and Andrew had been together a short while ago.

Oh, what did it matter! She was not interested in de Bouvier's messages. She wanted to know what had happened this time to take Lucian away from her.

Since his appointment in February, Lucian was always away. He was either at Whitehall or on a diplomatic mission that had to do with the future of the exiled French king.

If only they were already married. Then, when he worked late, he could come into her bedchamber and tell her what had put the gentlemen from Whitehall in a pother.

But the marriage could not take place until she turned one-and-twenty on the first of September. If it did take place at all.

If . . . ? For goodness' sake! Of course the wedding would take place. What an absolutely stupid notion to take into her head. She and Lucian would get married. Either on the second or on the third day of September.

Sophy gave herself a mental shake and blamed Louis de Bouvier for her odd humor. When he shed his pessimism, he must have dropped it on her. But a mental shaking did not rid her of apprehension. The period of waiting for her wedding day stretched out of all proportion.

July to September. Two months. In that time, her cousin Jonathan could hatch more objections why Sophy, a Bancroft of Rose Manor, should not give herself in wedlock to the Whig Viscount Northrop.

Three

The pessimism couldn't last. It wasn't in Sophy's nature to be blue-deviled for long. The following morning, when a maid brought, besides a cup of chocolate, one red rose to her bed with "his lordship's compliments, miss," she smiled with delight. She knew it meant Lucian had already left again for Whitehall, but it was a beautiful, bright summer morning, and he had sent her a rose.

Quickly, she washed, dressed in a cool, high-waisted muslin gown, and ran a comb through her short curls. After Lucian's departure from Dolwyn House she had been unable to eat, even though the late supper set out in the dining room consisted of many of her favorite delicacies. Now she was famished, and a cup of chocolate did nothing to alleviate hunger pangs.

Since her first day as governess in Payne House, Sophy had been expected to take luncheon and dinner in the family dining room. Breakfast she usually shared with Nurse Appleby and the children, Philip, George, and Lucy, in the nursery. But now the children were at Simpson Hall, their home in Kent, which, during their parents' absence, was managed by their paternal grandparents. They would stay at Simpson Hall until the end of the summer.

Or until the beacons on the Channel coast warned of the approach of an invasion fleet.

Meanwhile, Sophy was at liberty to order breakfast served on a tray in her room—as was Miss Addie's custom—or she could help herself from an array of covered dishes in the breakfast parlor. She infinitely preferred the latter. At least, it gave her a slight, a very slight chance of seeing Lucian before he set out for the Foreign Office.

This morning, as she had known from the appearance of the rose with her chocolate, Lucian was not in his place at the head of the table. She had known it, yet was disappointed. The heart, unfortunately, does not acknowledge what the mind perceives so clearly.

However, Andrew was there, which surprised her a little. Andrew Payne had a very nice set of chambers in York Street, and since the location was close to Whitehall she had not expected to see him at Payne House this morning.

"Hello, Andrew. Chaperoning again?"

She was referring to his own teasing explanation for staying more often in his brother's house than in his own chambers. Straight-faced but with laughter dancing in his blue eyes, Andrew had told Sophy she needed all the chaperonage she could get to still the tongues that wagged over her unorthodox position in Lucian's household. Indeed, there were two or three wagging tongues, but the majority of the *ton*, although labeling Sophy an eccentric young lady, had accepted her without a fuss.

Pushing aside a sheaf of papers he'd been studying, her future brother-in-law bid her a good morning.

"Didn't think to see you downstairs so early," he said, watching her lazily through half closed eyes as she helped herself to scrambled egg, grilled tomato, and a slice of ham. "Or didn't you stay at the ball after we left?"

"We stayed until two. That was long enough for me, and Miss Addie looked tired."

Sophy took her customary seat opposite Andrew. She thought that he looked tired, too. At least, his eyes did, circled by shadows and reddened—by lack of sleep?

"When did you and Lucian get home?"

"An hour ago." He gave her a boyish grin. "Just in time to shave and change clothes."

She poured tea for herself, more coffee for Andrew. "Lucian is still in town, I hope. He isn't being sent abroad on a diplomatic mission?"

"I doubt he'll be sent anywhere," Andrew said cheerfully. Too cheerfully to reassure Sophy. "The way Castlereagh is talking, any mission we'll undertake will be of an expeditionary nature."

"That's just what Kit has been hoping for."

"Aye. Castlereagh is wanting to send expeditionary forces into Hanover, South America, and Portugal. Kit's regiment may be one he's planning to order abroad."

Sophy pushed a sliver of ham around her plate. She wondered if Andrew understood enough about the matter to know for certain that diplomatic agents weren't sent along with the expeditionary forces.

Before the bleak prospect of Lucian in South America or Portugal could take hold of her mind, she was diverted by the rap of the front door knocker.

Andrew pulled a watch from his waistcoat pocket. "Eight o'clock. Sir Jermyn offered to take me up in his carriage on his way to the Admiralty. You can say what you want about him, but he is punctual."

"Quite a feat, indeed," Sophy said wryly, "since one of his major faults is absentmindedness."

"That's not as bad as his loose tongue. At times I wish—" Andrew shook his head.

As she watched him, it occurred to Sophy that he looked more troubled and perturbed than tired. And his earlier cheerfulness had rung false, as though he were putting too much effort into a grin, a hearty tone.

She had no time to question him. Footsteps approached in the hallway. A moment later, Waring, Lucian's stooped, white-haired butler, ushered Sir Jermyn Leister into the breakfast parlor.

"Your ale will be up directly, Sir Jermyn," said Waring before closing the door. There was no need to have a third place set. At Payne House, the breakfast table was always laid to accommodate early morning visitors.

Sir Jermyn Leister, a member of the Board of Admiralty and Andrew's immediate superior, had the reputation of a rake and, despite a balding pate and protruding stomach, still fancied himself a ladies' man. He pinched Sophy's cheek, told her she was looking devilishly pretty and Northrop was a lucky young dog. Finally, he lowered himself onto the chair beside her.

Andrew, as familiar with Sir Jermyn's preferences as the baronet was with the casual hospitality of Payne House, filled a plate with a variety of meats.

He set the food before Sir Jermyn just as a footman carried in a tray loaded with a foaming tankard, pots of tea and coffee, and a silver rack stacked with fresh toast.

The footman had barely left when Sir Jermyn, a forkful of deviled kidneys arrested halfway between plate and mouth, turned to Sophy.

"You've had some experience with thievery and the like, Miss Sophy. What do you make of the affair?"

"What affair?" Sophy perked instantly. "If you're speaking of last night, sir, I don't know anything. Lucian had time for only a few words—"

"Aye, 'twas a demmed uncomfortable time at Dolwyn House. What with Mr. Pitt breathing down our necks and Lord Dolwyn threatening to resign from the Board of Admiralty if something isn't done right away, Northrop had no choice but to take immediate leave of you."

"No, indeed," she said, more confused than enlightened. Something disastrous must have happened, or the Prime Minister would not have involved himself in Admiralty affairs.

She gave Andrew a questioning look, but his gaze was fixed on Sir Jermyn. One might think he was trying to will Sir Jermyn not to talk—which was strange, since Andrew and Lucian discussed such matters in front of her. Even sensitive matters. They knew she would never, not willingly, not carelessly or even unwittingly, divulge their business to a soul.

Sophy had always been curious, had never denied or tried to hide her inquisitive nature, and Andrew's behavior only served to whet her curiosity.

"I don't understand, Sir Jermyn. Lucian's work is

at the Foreign Office. What does he have to do with the Admiralty or the Prime Minister?"

"Mr. Pitt has ordered the Whitehall departments to work together," said Andrew, seeing that Sir Jermyn had just taken a mouthful of sirloin.

"Aye." The baronet washed down the meat with a draft of ale. "Too many documents disappearing, and everyone too busy blaming everyone else to do much about it. So Pitt wants the bickering stopped and the traitor caught."

Sophy—indeed, anyone who cared to read the papers or listen to the gentlemen in question— knew of the "mislaid" documents and the skirmishes between the Horse Guards, the Admiralty, the War Office, and the Foreign Office. Skirmishes that had been going on for time immemorial and did not explain the Prime Minister's interference at this point or Lord Dolwyn's threat to resign.

And why had Sir Jermyn started the conversation off with an allusion to her past experience as a thief-taker? Could he want her help?

Again, Sophy shot a look at Andrew. *He* could give her the gist of the matter in a few concise sentences. But he only raised a brow and shrugged.

She turned back to the baronet. "Sir Jermyn, can you tell me what happened?"

He dabbed a handkerchief to his brow. "Miss Sophy, three days ago, we received Admiral Nelson's latest dispatches. For some reason or other, Nelson believes that Villeneuve, who escaped him in the West Indies, is headed for Toulon."

"Toulon?" Sophy's brow wrinkled. "That's the harbor on the east coast of France, where Villeneuve first broke through our blockade. Why would the French admiral return there when he's supposed to escort Napoleon's invasion fleet across the Channel?"

Andrew made a sound that might have been a cough but, more likely, was a choke of laughter hastily suppressed.

"Beg your pardon," he murmured. "You sounded just like a governess."

"I *am* a governess," she said rather stiffly.

At any other time, she would have laughed with him. But this morning, she did not understand Andrew. One moment, he was his old cheerful self, and the next, he looked distinctly uncomfortable with Sir Jermyn's disclosures.

"And even if I were not a teacher," she told Andrew, "I would still be capable of logical thinking." She transferred her gaze to Sir Jermyn. "If Lucian were here, he'd confirm that it was my sharp mind he first admired."

She did not add that, at the time, Lucian's admiration of her mental powers had failed to please. To the governess who was beginning to acknowledge a *tendre* for her employer, Lucian's praise had felt like a slap in the face rather than a compliment.

"Just so," Sir Jermyn said absently. Sophy doubted he had listened to anything she or Andrew said.

Discovering his tankard empty, the baronet asked for a cup of coffee. Adding cream and sugar, he said peevishly, "I don't pretend to understand Nelson. The dispatches state that he has left the West Indies to chase Villeneuve around Gibraltar and to Toulon. But, devil a bit! Captain Bettesworth— he commands the brig Nelson sent home to deliver the reports—*saw* the French fleet."

He stopped for breath and a sip of his coffee.

"They have Spanish gunboats with them, too. And the course they've set is heading them for the Bay of Biscay."

The west coast of France.

This time, Sophy did not speak the thought aloud.

Andrew did, adding, "A hop and a skip to the Channel. If Villeneuve isn't intercepted . . . if he gets to Boulogne . . ."

Invasion.

The lack of an escort was the only reason Napoleon hadn't sent his great army across the Channel yet. The flat-bottomed invasion craft, designed for troop transport and a beach landing on the English coast, were not equipped to fight if the English resisted the invasion, which they most assuredly would.

Napoleon needed gunboats. He had men-of-war lying in Brest, but they were blockaded by British vessels and hadn't been able to stick a nose out of the harbor. Admiral Villeneuve was Napoleon's only hope.

"Are you saying, sir, that Lord Nelson's dispatches have disappeared?" asked Sophy. "And have not been returned?"

"Aye. They've been missing since day before yesterday from Lord Dolwyn's office. And I'll wager a pony, a French agent has them now."

She shook her head. "But, Sir Jermyn, I don't see the harm in that. If anything, Nelson's report will make the French believe we're unaware of their movements. Seems to me it couldn't have been better if we had planned it."

Again, the baronet mopped his brow. "It could have been called a stroke of good luck if, along with

Nelson's reports, the drafts of Lord Barham's reply to the admiral hadn't disappeared as well."

"Gracious," Sophy said weakly. This was a fine kettle of fish.

She ventured another look at Andrew. He did not meet her eyes. The only indication of his feelings was the tight white line around his mouth.

"And if that isn't enough," Sir Jermyn said morosely, "there's the muddle about Lieutenant Marston. He was supposed to leave at daybreak to take a dispatch to Bournemouth—Lord Barham's orders for Admiral Calder to intercept Villeneuve."

Sophy sipped her tea, which was cold by now, and she hated cold tea. But pouring a fresh cup might break her concentration.

"Sir Jermyn." Sophy took a deep breath. "You mentioned my past expertise in catching a thief." He had not phrased it precisely that way, but Sophy wasn't one to split hairs. "Sir, do you want me to catch the document thief for the Admiralty?"

"The thief," Andrew cut in harshly, "is a traitor. And a murderer."

In the sudden stillness, Sophy heard her own sharply drawn breath.

"Lieutenant Peter Marston was killed last night," said Andrew. "Stabbed to death."

Four

The body of Naval Lieutenant Peter Marston, age twenty-four, had been found in St. James's about a quarter to eleven on the night of the Dolwyn ball. It was found in York Street at the corner of Jermyn Street, near the narrow side gate of Brompton's Livery Stables. Marston had been stabbed through the heart.

He was discovered by Horace, a former marine employed by the Admiralty as a messenger and general factotum who also served as Andrew Payne's gentleman's gentleman in the York Street chambers. On Horace's shout, two Charleys patrolling Jermyn Street came running. Setting one to guard the body and sending the other to the Admiralty, Horace hurried to Payne House to inform Andrew. Andrew, in turn, set out instantly for Dolwyn House to notify Sir Jermyn Leister and Lord Barham, the First Lord of Admiralty.

The dispatch from Lord Barham to Admiral Calder—orders to sail immediately and to intercept Admiral Villeneuve off Ferrol, Spain—was not on Marston's body. Neither was the document in Lord Barham's office safe, to which Marston had access. Nor was it found in the lieutenant's lodgings in St. Martin's Lane.

These were the facts as Sophy learned them from Andrew and Sir Jermyn Leister. Before she had recovered from the shocking news of Peter Marston's violent death, the gentlemen took a hurried leave.

They were all at sixes and sevens at the Admiralty, said Sir Jermyn. Lord Barham was determined to find the man who had betrayed and killed Lieutenant Marston. Whether the traitor had personally stabbed Marston or whether he had merely pointed him out to a French agent was immaterial. He must be found before he could do further harm.

Shaken, Sophy stood in the open front door. Her gaze was fixed on the carriage as it rattled off toward Whitehall, but her mind was on Peter Marston.

She had known him only the few short weeks of the London Season. He limped severely and did not dance, but Sophy as well as other young ladies had often "saved" a dance, then sat out and enjoyed a conversation with the young naval lieutenant.

He had a charming smile, and Sophy had never seen him in ill humor. But, perhaps because she had accepted the responsibility of mothering and raising two younger sisters when she was only six years old, she had learned to be more observant than other young ladies. Every now and then, when she talked with Peter Marston, she had caught a shadow in his eyes—bitterness or frustration, or both. Dark emotions which the most cheerful smile could not quite hide.

Sophy was skillful at drawing people out, and as, bit by bit, she learned about Peter Marston's life, she began to understand his frustration. He was a man of action.

He had gone to sea at age fourteen. Like Horatio Nelson, he had been made lieutenant at nineteen. His future looked promising. Sailing under Captain Cumming on the *Russell*, Peter Marston saw his own captaincy well within reach during the Baltic expedition. But he lost a foot in the engagement that became known as the Battle of Copenhagen and was invalided home.

Recovery was slow. Marston, however, was determined to master his handicap. On April 2, 1802, exactly one year after his injury, he resumed active duty with a wooden foot strapped to his ankle.

He stayed at sea nine months, then volunteered for a half-pay post at the naval yard in Bournemouth. Peter Marston had finally acknowledged that, especially during severe weather, he was more hindrance than help to his commander and crew.

In May of 1804, Lord Melville, a distant cousin of Peter Marston's mother, offered him a post as secretary-cum-aide in the office of First Lord of Admiralty—a post, Peter learned later, created by combining the duties of a bumbling old commodore on the First Lord's staff, who had finally agreed to retire, and the duties of a senior clerk, who had been shuffled into a different office. Pay was a pittance, and the only action Peter could hope for was a ride now and then to Bournemouth or some other naval yard with dispatches from the First Lord of Admiralty.

But at least London held the promise of relief from total, utter boredom. "My mother and two of my sisters live in Bloomsbury," Peter had told Sophy. "And Melville has been dashed kind. Sponsored me so I could join White's and Brooks's."

The Marston family background was impeccable, and Lord Melville also took the trouble to introduce his young kinsman to several society hostesses, who welcomed him with open arms. Unattached young gentlemen, especially when they were as personable as Peter Marston, were in great demand for making up the numbers at the dinner table.

Even when Lord Barham succeeded Viscount Melville as First Lord of Admiralty, Peter had no need to worry about getting sent back to some naval yard or other. Barham showed no desire to dismiss his predecessor's *protégé*.

No, Peter Marston had no reason for complaint. And he never did complain. He was unfailingly polite and cheerful, universally liked by the ladies and gentlemen of the *ton* as well as by his colleagues at the Admiralty. Most likely, no one but Sophy ever suspected the frustration behind his charming smile, the young man's hankering for action.

And now Lieutenant Peter Marston was dead. Murdered. For the sake of a piece of paper—the dispatch from Lord Barham to Admiral Calder that was missing?

Emerging from deep thought, Sophy hugged her arms to her chest. *Murder.* A chilling word. It raised goose bumps on the warmest of July mornings.

Not too long ago, Payne House had been plagued by a thief who turned into a cold-blooded killer when threatened with exposure. Sophy remembered the distress caused not only by the murder itself, the death of Miss Addie's faithful old abigail, but by the ever-widening circles of suspicion that had rippled through Payne House. Sophy had been instrumental in catching the thief and murderer, but not until the very end had she been certain she was pursuing the right man.

With Peter Marston's murder, suspicion would

run rampant in the stately chambers of the Admiralty. The Whitehall building would be a most uncomfortable place until the traitor was caught.

Sophy was about to close the door when she saw a hackney coach pulling up in front of the house. Lost in dark thoughts, she had neither seen nor heard its approach.

Curious—after all, it wasn't nine o'clock yet; rather early for a caller—she waited while the jarvey clambered down from the box, assisted his passenger to alight, and, after pocketing his fare, took off without delay.

Mademoiselle de Bouvier, left standing at the curb, looked uncertainly at Sophy.

Uncertainty was not a characteristic the young Frenchwoman usually displayed. In fact, Sophy could not recall a single instance prior to this morning when Véronique had been less than poised and self-confident.

"Good morning, Mademoiselle de Bouvier. Won't you come inside?"

Slowly, Véronique mounted the steps. "I should like to speak with Mr. Payne. Is he here this morning?"

"He was, but I'm afraid you've missed him." Sophy couldn't help but think that Véronique had been rash in letting the hackney go before making sure Andrew was indeed at Payne House. "He left for the Admiralty about ten or fifteen minutes ago."

"Oh." A *moue* accompanied the sigh. And yet, considering that she had quite failed in her objective, Véronique did not seem half as disappointed as might be expected.

Prompted as much by curiosity as by courtesy, Sophy once more asked Mademoiselle de Bouvier to come inside. "You could write a note and, if it's urgent, I'll have someone take it to the Admiralty."

"You are very kind." A sparkle entered Véronique's dark eyes. She stepped past Sophy into the marble-tiled hall. "But, in truth, my business with Mr. Payne is not so very urgent. It is just that Louis was called out of town, and he believes he forgot to mention it to Mr. Payne. They planned to attend some auction or other on Friday, and Louis fears he may not be back in time."

"It must be the auction at Tattersalls. Andrew has his eyes on a matched pair."

A memory tugged at Sophy's mind. Louis de Bouvier at the Dolwyn ball. He knew then that he was going out of town. He and Véronique both mentioned it. And Louis had reminded Véronique to give his message to Andrew—who had been with him just moments earlier.

And a message to Peter Marston, who was already dead then. Of course, no one but the gentlemen from Whitehall had known this at the time. Even now, the young naval lieutenant's death would not be widely known. Sophy wished she had asked Sir Jermyn if the murder was to be kept quiet for the present.

Pensive, she watched as Mademoiselle de Bouvier stopped in front of the mirror, adjusted her dainty silk-and-lace hat, and twisted a lock of her hair, which was quite as dark as Sophy's. But while Sophy's hair was merely a plain dark brown, Véronique's had the same rich mahogany tint as her cousin Louis's. And Véronique was one of the few French ladies in London who did not wear the fashionable short crop but an elaborate coiffure of long curls.

Véronique smiled warmly. "Miss Bancroft, we have met and conversed several times. But there never is the time at a ball or at a *soirée* to get truly acquainted, is there?"

"No, indeed. One is forever interrupted."

"So, rather than waste time writing a note when, undoubtedly, I shall see Mr. Payne later today or tomorrow, I would much prefer to chat with you."

There was nothing to say but "How delightful."

And why, thought Sophy as she ushered her visitor into the sunny front parlor, do I suddenly have the feeling that mademoiselle has not failed in her objective after all?

Thirty minutes later, Sophy wondered if her ever-fertile imagination had run away with her.

Véronique had refused coffee and tea and immediately launched into the sort of insipid conversation Sophy had come to expect from morning callers, though not usually at nine of the clock. Véronique had chatted about the Dolwyn ball and the picnic planned by the Piercepoints two days hence in Richmond Park. She had talked about card parties and musical evenings, routs and drums and *soirées* until Sophy wished the children weren't in the country, so she might excuse herself with pressing duties on the nursery floor.

But, in thirty minutes, Véronique had not said a word or asked a single question that substantiated Sophy's notion that the Frenchwoman had come to Payne House specifically to see her. Neither could Sophy imagine what Véronique would want of her.

Mademoiselle de Bouvier did not usually seek female companionship. When Andrew had first

pointed her out to Sophy, Véronique had been surrounded by gentlemen—young and old, husbands
and bachelors. And whenever Sophy saw the young
lady afterward, it was always the same picture:
Véronique laughing and chatting with at least a half
dozen gentlemen.

Within Sophy's hearing, several ladies had described Véronique as a dreadful flirt. However, not
the starchiest matron accused her of impropriety.
Mademoiselle de Bouvier might laugh and flirt, but
she kept every gentleman at arm's length. Even Andrew Payne, who was head over heels in love with
her.

Sophy acknowledged a growing curiosity about
the Frenchwoman, and when Véronique's chatter
slowed, she said, "Your command of the English
language is admirable. How long have you lived in
this country, mademoiselle?"

If Véronique was surprised by the switch in topic,
she did not show it. She readily abandoned past
and future entertainments to explain that she had
come to England when she was only ten years old.

Her wide mouth curved in a smile. "And I was
very fortunate. *Mon père*, he is a farsighted man. He
sent much of his fortune to an English bank before
the outbreak of the revolution. So, when we finally
escaped in ninety-two, there was money to engage
a governess for me and a tutor for Louis."

"Then your cousin escaped with you?" asked
Sophy, quickly calculating Mademoiselle de Bouvier's age. Twenty-three. The same age as Andrew.

"But yes." Véronique gathered her gloves and
reticule. "Louis is an orphan. There was the
cholera, you see. His parents died when he was a
babe in arms. My parents had just been married,

and they took him in. Louis is a son to them, a brother to me."

She rose. Again the wide smile flashed. "He was fourteen when we arrived in England, had lost the child's ability to mimic. He very much dislikes having to acknowledge my superiority in anything, but he cannot deny that my English is less accented than his."

Sophy rose as well. "Your English is excellent and almost accent free. I congratulate you."

"Congratulations must go to my governess. But I need not explain to you, I think. You know the value of good teaching. You were the governess to Lord Northrop's wards before your betrothal, were you not?"

"I still am their governess. When Lady Simpson engaged me, she did so in the expectation that I would stay with her children until her return."

Véronique's dark eyes widened. "But I understand that Lord and Lady Simpson will not return until the end of the year at the soonest—from China, is it not?"

"Yes, they are in China."

"Then you will *not* be married at the end of the summer? You will still be—" Véronique broke off, looking uncomfortable. "Forgive me. I did not mean to appear curious or impertinent."

Sophy said nothing. The problems attached to her betrothal and wedding were no more Véronique's business than they were the Dowager Duchess of Wigmore's. She had ignored the nosy old duchess and her questions; she certainly would ignore the young Frenchwoman who had caught Andrew's fancy.

Véronique pulled on her gloves. "It has been a

pleasure visiting with you, Miss Bancroft. I have been wanting to get to know you. Mr. Payne, he thinks the world of you. And he made me curious, for he speaks of you quite often."

"He does?" Sophy wasn't certain she liked being a subject of discussion between Andrew and Mademoiselle de Bouvier.

"But yes. He says you are the most redoubtable young lady he knows. The only one to deal with his brother, who, I understand, is a very strong-willed gentleman. Except—"

"Except?" Sophy's voice was cool. She knew what Andrew must have said. That she dealt extremely well with Lucian . . . except when it came to the wedding date.

"I beg your pardon, Miss Bancroft. This morning, my tongue is running on like a fiddle stick. I have offended you, and I fear that anything I add in explanation will only make matters worse."

"Perhaps it will," Sophy admitted. "I am a little sensitive after the Dowager Duchess of Wigmore's catechism last night. I should not be, though."

"One cannot help one's feelings."

Something in the other woman's tone made Sophy take notice. The words were trite, but Véronique had spoken from the heart.

Again, Sophy was aware of curiosity. She could hardly ask about Véronique's feelings, though, after snubbing her for asking about the wedding, which was, after all, less private than one's feelings.

And what about the reason for the unusually early visit if the message to Andrew wasn't urgent? Or why Véronique had stayed—was it truly just to get acquainted?

Her eyes met Véronique's, dark and unfathomable. Mysterious. No wonder Andrew was head over heels and had no thought to spare for the not-at-all-mysterious Lady Jane.

"Is something the matter, Miss Bancroft? A smudge on my nose, perhaps?"

Mercurially, Sophy's mood lightened. "No, there's no smudge on your nose. I apologize for staring. I don't mean to, but I'm afraid that's what I often do when I'm preoccupied."

"If you're still distressed about what I said—"

"Lud! What a to-do I made about nothing. I know Andrew considers you a friend. No doubt, he told you that Lucian and I squabble like a pair of nursery brats over the wedding date. One insists on an even-numbered date. The other prefers the odds. It is so very silly, and I don't know why Andrew's talking about it should have upset me."

"Is it silly?" Véronique started for the parlor door. "At present, it sounds to me like a . . . comedy, perhaps? Comedy is very good between lovers. What you do not want is a Cheltenham tragedy."

"No, indeed."

But the notion of enacting Lucian a tragedy when next he brought up the question of the wedding date caught Sophy's fancy. He would certainly wish to shake her. He always wanted to shake her when she exasperated him. And then he always ended up kissing her.

Sophy opened the door and, seeing Miss Addie's sharp-faced little page skip across the hall toward the baize-covered kitchen door, called out to him.

"Skeet! Run along to Piccadilly, will you, and fetch a hackney for Mademoiselle de Bouvier."

The boy whisked off, returning with the desired conveyance in less time than it took Mademoiselle de Bouvier to thank Sophy once more for the opportunity to talk and get acquainted.

Descending the five steps from the front door to the street, Véronique stopped and looked over her shoulder.

"Miss Bancroft, I wonder if you can help me?"

Ah.

The sigh was inaudible but heartfelt. Sophy was gratified to know that her imagination had not run away with her. Véronique de Bouvier had indeed had a purpose for seeking her out.

Five

"Help you?" Sophy gave Véronique a speculative look. "Yes, of course I shall, if it is at all possible."

"I need a lady's escort for an errand I promised to perform. Can you spare the time to accompany me?"

"Now?"

"Yes. I promise you it will not take very long."

"I have time. More than enough. Just let me fetch my hat," said Sophy, disappearing into the house.

Sped on by curiosity, she raced up three flights of stairs to her chamber on the nursery floor. Reticule, gloves, hat—and she was on her way down again, tying the cherry-colored ribbons of the wide-brimmed straw hat beneath her left ear.

Mademoiselle de Bouvier was waiting in the hackney carriage. "There," said Sophy, joining her. "That didn't take long, did it?"

"No, indeed. And I am very grateful to you."

Nothing more was said until the jarvey had put up the steps and slammed the door.

"Miss Bancroft, you must be wondering why I turn to you for help."

"Not at all," Sophy said politely. She did wonder, but she was even more curious about the nature of the errand that required chaperonage. "I'm happy to oblige. Am I, perchance, accompanying you to an assignation?"

The pause before Véronique's reply was so slight that Sophy might have imagined it.

"No, Miss Bancroft. But it is an errand of some delicacy. I do not wish to trouble my mother, whose constitution is not strong. And—you must have noticed—I do not have a great number of lady friends upon whom I might call for assistance."

Sophy had noticed it. At social functions she had seen Véronique surrounded only by gentlemen. But didn't she have a female friend among the other *émigré* families?

A shout from the jarvey on the box, a crack of his whip, and with a jerk the carriage started to roll.

"As a matter of fact," said Sophy, bracing herself for further jolts of the extremely ill-sprung vehicle, "I'm not wondering so much why you chose me as your companion or why you would need a chaperone at all as I am wondering about *where* we are going."

"No farther than St. Martin's Lane."

Sophy did not move or betray in any other way that the street name had given her as nasty a jolt as the bumping of the hackney coach. Peter Marston's lodgings were in St. Martin's Lane.

"Louis was hoping to see Lieutenant Marston at the Dolwyn ball last night," said Véronique. "But since Peter—Lieutenant Marston did not make an appearance, Louis asked me to give him a message."

Sophy remembered it well. A message for Andrew and a message for Lieutenant Marston.

She also noticed the quick correction from "Peter" to "Lieutenant Marston." And she remembered that Peter Marston, along with Sir Jermyn

Leister, had generally made one of the crowd of gentlemen surrounding Mademoiselle de Bouvier.

"This message," she said. "It is, apparently, more urgent than the message to Andrew?"

"It is of the utmost importance. But I do not wish to disturb the lieutenant at the Admiralty where, I am sure, he must be at this time. You are acquainted with him, Miss Bancroft. I hoped you would not mind going with me to his chambers so I can leave Louis's note."

A note Peter Marston would never read.

Sophy was not often at a loss, but she did not know how to deal with the situation. If only she'd had the foresight to ask Sir Jermyn whether the Admiralty wanted Marston's death kept quiet for the present.

Misunderstanding the silence, Véronique said, "I was wrong. You *do* mind. I must beg your pardon. It is just that I believed it would be all right for you, the lady betrothed to the Viscount Northrop, to accompany me. But if you fear for your reputation—"

"Nonsense."

Sophy would not dance a third time with Kit Hawthorne, but playing chaperone to a young lady determined to visit a bachelor's lodgings was a different kettle of fish. Especially when that young lady had an urgent note for the gentleman. A dead man.

Turning on the hard seat, she faced Véronique. "It would have been so much simpler to hire a messenger to deliver your cousin's note. If you had told me, I could have sent Skeet, Miss Addie's page. He never turns down an opportunity to earn a penny."

"It is not the kind of note I could entrust to a messenger."

"No?" Beneath an overwhelming curiosity, Sophy was aware of a growing unease.

"Louis and Peter are friends." Véronique gave Sophy a sidelong look. "Every now and then, Louis picks up a tidbit of information that has come from France. He passes it on to Peter."

A part of Sophy's mind noted that Véronique had once more used the naval lieutenant's first name, and that it sounded as though she was quite used to calling him Peter.

The other, more active part of her mind dealt with the startling bit of news Véronique had imparted. Louis de Bouvier spying for Lieutenant Marston!

Louis made no secret of his feelings about the upstart Emperor Napoleon, but Sophy had categorized him as a dandified fribble—charming but useless. It was difficult to imagine the elegant young Frenchman doing something as potentially dangerous as passing information.

Was Lord Barham aware of this? Or Sir Jermyn Leister and Andrew? Or had Peter Marston withheld the name of his informant?

"Mademoiselle, should you be telling me all this?"

"I believe you are a safe person to tell. Soon you will be the wife of a gentleman working with the Foreign Secretary and the sister-in-law of Mr. Payne, who, Louis told me, decodes French dispatches and documents intercepted by English spies."

"Your cousin's note may contain vital information. News, perhaps, of Napoleon's invasion plans. We should take it straight to Whitehall."

"No!"

Sophy's eyes widened at Véronique's vehemence. "I apologize, Miss Bancroft. I did not mean to shout at you. It is just that Peter is adamant about not seeing Louis or me at the Admiralty."

Sophy's mouth was dry. Peter Marston would never again be adamant about anything.

"He says it is too dangerous." Véronique hesitated. "Everyone going in and out of the Admiralty is watched by French agents. You are aware, of course, that London harbors a number of these villains?"

Sophy nodded. Lucian and Andrew had talked about the French agents more than once. When she asked why they weren't arrested or expelled, Lucian had explained that it was better to let the agents stay, to keep them under surveillance. A known enemy presented little danger. It was the unknown agent or spy who did damage.

But, no matter how well watched a French agent was, he could undoubtedly find a way to kill an *émigré* suspected of collaborating with the English.

And if Louis de Bouvier was in danger, so would be the man who had engaged the *émigré's* services, Peter Marston. Perhaps Peter had not been killed for the dispatches; their disappearance could have been incidental. Perhaps he had been killed so he could not meet Louis de Bouvier at Dolwyn House.

But if someone had known Louis was waiting to pass information to Peter, wouldn't that someone have killed Louis?

Sophy gave an inaudible sniff. She was getting fanciful. There was no point speculating until she had spoken with Lucian. Or with Andrew.

"Miss Bancroft, do you wish that I tell the driver to turn back?"

Recalled to the matter of immediate concern, Sophy looked out the window. They were still on Piccadilly, approaching Coventry Street. In another ten or fifteen minutes they would be in St. Martin's Lane.

Ten minutes to decide whether she ought to inform Mademoiselle de Bouvier of Peter Marston's death.

"I'll go with you." Sophy turned back to Véronique. "If I don't, I wager you'll set out on your own as soon as you put me down at Payne House."

Smiling slightly, Véronique said, "I think, Miss Bancroft, that we could easily become friends."

And Sophy, who never had a friend her own age—unless one counted two younger sisters—warmed toward the woman she had been prepared to dislike for the sake of Lady Jane Hawthorne. When Kit had introduced his sister to Sophy, he had expressed the hope that the two young ladies would become friends. But to Sophy, Jane was another "little sister" to be guided and protected. Véronique de Bouvier did not give the impression that she needed guidance or protection. She could, indeed, be a friend.

But a friend deserved frankness. Honesty. A friend ought to be told that her errand was in vain. It was the memory of Andrew, his obvious discomfort when Sir Jermyn had talked so freely about Peter Marston's murder and the missing dispatches, that kept Sophy quiet.

They drove in silence until the hackney turned south on St. Martin's Lane and approached the corner of Chandos Street.

"So many carriages," said Véronique, staring out the window. "All in front of the house where Peter is lodging. Surely no one is entertaining at this time of day?"

The hackney slowed, and Sophy switched to the

opposite seat. She put her face next to Véronique's. The first carriage she saw had emblazoned on its door the coat of arms of the viscounts Northrop.

Lucian here! What did it mean? She also recognized in the impressive line of vehicles Sir Jermyn Leister's carriage.

The hackney stopped. Véronique looped the drawstring of her reticule over her wrist and gathered her skirts preparatory to alighting.

"Mademoiselle." Sophy reached for the young Frenchwoman's hand. She could not let her face the gentlemen from Whitehall totally unprepared. "There is something you must know before—"

The door of the hackney was wrenched open. Not by the jarvey, but by Sophy's betrothed.

"Good morning, Sophy." Lucian's voice was polite, but she had learned to watch his eyes. There was nothing polite in the harassed look he gave her. "May I inquire what brought you to St. Martin's Lane?"

"Not *what*, Lucian. *Who*. Mademoiselle de Bouvier asked me to accompany her."

Only then did he pay attention to the second young lady in the hackney. He bowed but turned back to Sophy almost immediately.

"My dear, was this wise? I understand Sir Jermyn explained the situation to you."

Sophy gave back stare for stare, willing Lucian to understand. "I did not know if the situation was to be kept quiet. Also, I did not think anyone would be here since Sir Jermyn said the rooms have already been searched. Pray give me a moment to prepare Mademoiselle de Bouvier."

"Prepare me for what?" Véronique, who had been looking anxiously from one to the other, spoke sharply. Her dark eyes fastened on Lucian. "Something has happened, has it not? To Peter!"

"I'm afraid so, mademoiselle. And I wish Sophy had stopped you from coming here."

Véronique blanched. Her hand, still lying beneath Sophy's, clenched.

"He is dead," she said with a calm and a certainty as chilling as they were unnerving. She did not reproach Sophy for not telling her. She did not even look at Sophy, but at Lucian.

"You killed him. Your bloody government killed Peter. *Sacrebleu!* What a waste of a good man."

Six

"Your bloody government killed Peter."

Sophy could not get the accusation out of her mind. It made no sense. Yet all day long, the words pursued her.

Véronique must have been badly shaken to have used such strong language. And if Peter Marston had meant more to her than a contact at the Admiralty, her mind might have been addled by pain and distress—which would explain why she accused the English government rather than a French agent of killing the naval lieutenant.

Sophy had not been able to speak to Véronique that morning. Andrew had appeared beside his brother, helped Véronique from the hackney, and led her toward the entrance to Peter Marston's lodging house.

Lucian, ignoring Sophy's questions, had paid off the hackney, bundled his betrothed into his own carriage, and ordered Samuel Trueblood, his trusted coachman, to take her straight back to Payne House. Fast.

It was insufferable to be treated thus by the man who claimed to love her. Infamous! Lucian must know that she had taken an interest in Mademoiselle de Bouvier and that she would have questions about the investigation into Peter Marston's death. She would certainly give Lucian a piece of her mind as soon as he came home.

Unfortunately for Sophy, Lucian did not return to Payne House until late that night. Miss Addie had retired. Sophy, having worn a path in the nap of the fine old Axminster carpet in the morning room, had sunk into a soft, deep chair. Behind her, the French doors leading into the garden stood open to admit cool night air delicately scented with jasmine and clove pinks. A lamp on the table beside her cast a pool of warm yellow light on a stack of fashion plates in her hands, but she gazed only absently at the drawings of bridal gowns.

The door opened. Lucian, looking utterly weary, paused on the threshold.

"Lucian! I thought you'd never come home."

His mouth relaxed and curved in the special smile, the smile that was only for her. "My love. You waited up for me. It's the best thing that happened to me this whole bloody day."

The best? His smile had softened her. His words made her glow. Heedless of the fashion plates tumbling to the floor, Sophy rushed into his waiting arms. For the moment, indignation was forgotten, questions faded to insignificance.

Holding her tight, he claimed her mouth possessively. But, perhaps, it was she who clung with such possessive ardor; she who did not want the kiss to end.

"Lud, Sophy!" He cupped her face with unsteady hands. "We must persuade your cousin to agree to an early marriage. I don't want to wait until September."

"Neither do I." She smiled. "Would we still squabble over an odd- or even-numbered day?"

His hands slid to her shoulders. He shook her gently, then kissed her again. "What do you say to July twenty-three? I'm willing to accept the two in that date as my even number. And you'll have your three."

"Ever the diplomat. And I was so looking forward to convincing you that odd numbers are luckier than even."

"I'd never have believed you could be superstitious. My love, you're a constant delight. But I'll prove you wrong."

His grip tightened. "You will write to Jonathan? Or, better yet, go to Rose Manor and speak to him."

"If I visited Rose Manor, I'd only make matters worse. Jonathan and I cannot spend five minutes in each other's company without coming to cuffs."

"Even if you tried?"

She sighed. "Alas."

Fluffing the tiny puffed sleeves of her gown, which had taken the brunt of Lucian's ardent grip, she gave him a sidelong look. "Besides, if we got married now, I might find myself deserted on my wedding night."

His brow clouded. Once again, he looked weary and older than his six-and-twenty years.

"I know," he said. "The timing is damnable. Villeneuve's escape from Nelson . . . Marston's death . . . they couldn't have happened at a worse time. King Louis and the Comte d'Artois are once again at loggerheads. These past ten days alone, three messengers arrived from Mittau with royal *communiqués*. Or, perhaps, I should say royal complaints."

And Lucian would no more back out of his commitments at the Foreign Office than Sophy would desert her post as governess. Even married to Lucian, she would continue to teach his niece and nephews until Lord and Lady Simpson returned from China.

She no longer desired to give Lucian a piece of her mind for sending her home earlier that day, but she still wanted to know the facts. All of them.

"Lucian, what happened this morning? Why were you in St. Martin's Lane? And why did you send me home? You let Véronique stay, didn't you? Else you wouldn't have paid off the hackney. Did you question her? What did Véronique say?"

Dryly, Lucian answered the last of the barrage of questions. "She demanded another hackney to take her home."

It was such a contrast to what Sophy had expected, she couldn't help it. She gave a choke of laughter.

After a moment, Lucian's mouth curved in a reluctant grin. He clasped Sophy's hand. "Walk with me in the garden."

Stepping out into the sweet-scented night, Sophy said, "Véronique was badly shaken. Did Andrew explain to her that it was most likely a French agent who killed Peter Marston?"

"No. For the time being, Peter's death will be blamed on footpads."

"But there's no question that it was not an attack by footpads? *The Times* pointed out only yesterday how brash they have become in the St. James's district, roaming the streets in bands of four and five like the Mohock gangs of old."

"No question at all. Peter still wore his signet ring and watch, and he carried a purse with seventy guineas. No footpad would have left such loot behind."

"Suppose someone came along before the thugs had time to rob him?"

"I doubt a passerby would have slowed or stopped a robbery. The footpads know that the ordinary citizen is afraid of them. The watchmen in St. James's are going about in pairs now, but even they hesitate to intervene."

Sophy gripped Lucian's hand more tightly. It was dark in the garden. As was so often the case, the moon and stars were hidden by the haze of smoke and soot that on a windless day sat like a canopy over the city. St. James's with its gentlemen's clubs and its gaming hells would be dark, too. Any gentleman abroad at night in that area would most likely be in his cups and not alert to danger. Ideal conditions for footpads.

Or for a French spy who—for whatever reason, to stop his quarry from going to Dolwyn House or to stop him from carrying dispatches to Bournemouth—wanted to kill Lord Barham's aide.

"Lucian, what was Lieutenant Marston doing in St. James's? Surely he wouldn't have visited a gaming house when he was supposed to leave for Bournemouth at dawn?"

They had reached the gazebo in the far right corner of the garden. Instead of answering her question, Lucian asked, "Are you tired? Shall we sit down?"

She looked at him but could distinguish no more than the outline of his face. "How can I be tired after sitting at home all day? Are you trying to divert me?"

"No. And if I were, I would hardly admit it." He let go of her hand, but only to slip an arm around her waist. "My dear Sophy, you're far too suspicious. Pray remember that, above all, a *fiancé* deserves trust."

"Yes, Lucian," she replied meekly and, without pause, repeated her earlier question. "Would Peter Marston have visited a gambling establishment on the eve of a strenuous ride? At least, I assume he would have ridden to Bournemouth. He told me more than once that he disliked coach travel."

"He planned to ride."

Lucian did not again suggest that they sit in the gazebo but continued along the graveled path.

He said, "Did Sir Jermyn tell you where in St. James's Peter Marston's body was found?"

"Near the side entrance of some livery stable at the corner of—" Her breath caught.

"Yes," said Lucian. "At the corner of York and Jermyn Streets."

"Lud! Why didn't I see it before? Peter Marston was in St. James's because he tried to see Andrew! Only Andrew wasn't in his York Street chambers. He was at the Dolwyn ball. No, wait. At that time he was here, wasn't he?"

"Who knows? I find it impossible to keep up with Andrew. But Horace seemed to think he was here. When Peter called at the York Street chambers around ten o'clock, Horace directed him here. Only, Peter asked to be let into the study to write a note first. Horace supplied him with pen and ink and a few minutes later showed Peter out again."

"And then Horace found him dead at a quarter to eleven."

Sophy's mind whirled. There seemed to be a great number of notes, dispatches, and messages involved in this affair.

"What did Peter say? Did he suspect something?

Perhaps he noticed that someone followed him and he wanted to ask Andrew for help."

"He did not confide in Horace, and the note told us nothing we didn't already know. Peter wrote only that he was leaving for Bournemouth in the morning and expected to be back Friday afternoon."

"Oh." A wave of disappointment washed over her. And sadness. For some reason, knowing what Peter Marston's last movements had been made his death so much worse . . . as though it could have been avoided.

What a waste of a good man. Those had been Véronique's words. Sophy could only agree. Peter Marston would be missed.

"He was such a nice young man. And I don't understand," she added crossly and quite irrelevantly, "why I didn't immediately realize he must have come from Andrew's chambers when he was killed."

"Perhaps," Lucian suggested gently, "you were too shaken by the news of his death."

He stopped and drew her into the shelter of his arms. "I promise you, we'll do everything in our power to find his killer."

"I'll help."

"My love, this is a government affair."

"I am aware of that."

"The most experienced agents have been called in to conduct the investigation."

She nestled closer against his chest. "I shan't interfere with anyone."

Lucian did not reply immediately, but she could feel him tense.

"Sophy, you mustn't get involved."

"I want to be involved." She pushed away from him. "Dash it, Lucian! I *liked* Peter Marston. Besides, Véronique drew me into the affair when she asked me to accompany her to St. Martin's Lane."

"Sophy!" Lucian's tone was ominous.

She was not to be quelled. "I certainly plan to cultivate Véronique's company. And Louis de Bouvier's, too. If you had not been so eager to be rid of me this morning, I could have told you that Louis was in the habit of supplying Peter Marston with bits of news from France. Véronique was carrying a note from Louis to Peter."

"Mademoiselle de Bouvier was spinning you a yarn."

Sophy did not want to believe it. But having to choose between Lucian's and Véronique's word was no choice at all.

"Are you saying there was no note from Louis to Peter?"

She sensed rather than saw his shrug.

"There may have been," he said dismissively. "We wanted to question Mademoiselle de Bouvier but didn't get a chance. She broke down. Ran the gamut from hysterical tears to swooning. Andrew took her home."

"It must have been an act! I cannot imagine Véronique indulging in a fit of hysterics. If only you had let me stay to talk to her. If she was telling the truth about having information for Peter, she and Louis may be in danger."

"Sophy, Peter Marston never received information from Louis de Bouvier. Or from Véronique. Or from anyone else."

"How can you be so certain? Peter may have kept the name of his informant secret."

"He might not have disclosed his source to the Board of Admiralty, but he certainly would have passed on the news he received. Believe me, Sophy. Peter Marston never collected information from anyone."

Sophy stared at the rose bushes behind Lucian and noted absently that the buds were thick enough to be noticeable in the dark. Another week, and the roses would be in full bloom.

She had to believe Lucian. He wouldn't make a statement without being certain of the facts.

But why had Véronique lied? And why, if she did not want to disclose the true nature of her errand, had she told such a senseless, utterly foolish lie? What did she want at Peter Marston's lodgings if she did not carry an urgent message from Louis?

And what had Lucian been about? And Andrew, Sir Jermyn, and the other Whitehall officials whose carriages were lined up in St. Martin's Lane?

Lucian watched her as she stood quite still, head cocked as though she were listening intently. It was a pose he had previously observed, during that harrowing time several months ago when she had plunged headlong into the investigation of theft and murder at Payne House. Seeing her thus made him feel decidedly uneasy.

He did not for an instant consider that she might be listening to the faint night sounds stirring in the garden. He knew her inquisitive, pertinacious nature too well. Despite his discouragement to involve herself in the Peter Marston affair, Sophy was already forming questions and weaving schemes that would, if he could but read her mind, turn his hair white. And her first question would be about the government assembly in St. Martin's Lane. He'd wager a pony on it.

His Sophy. Clever. Stubborn. Exasperating.

Adorable. His love and delight. And—memories of that other, earlier murder investigation revived—his despair.

Yet he wouldn't want her changed. Not for all the ambassadorships in the British Empire.

He leaned forward and kissed the tip of her pert nose. "A penny for your thoughts."

She looked at him. Even though he could not see her expression, he knew there would be that certain look in her eyes, a look that was as intent as it was mischievous.

"You'd be paying for something you already know."

"I was afraid of that."

There was a moment of silence.

"You don't want to tell me why you were at Peter Marston's lodging house? Why you bundled me off?" she asked, hurt. Then, with a pretense of indifference, "Or is it that you *cannot* tell me?"

"If I believed for an instant that it would keep you out of the affair I'd be tempted to say yes."

"Lucian, don't tease. You know very well that, if it's not a state secret, I'll hear about it sooner or later from Sir Jermyn."

"Even if it *were* a state secret," he said wryly.

"Well?" She started walking back toward the house. "What were you all doing in St. Martin's Lane? Did you find the missing dispatch in Peter's rooms after all?"

"No, Sophy." He easily caught up with her. "We found the place in shambles and Peter's old servant dead. Stabbed."

Seven

In the dark front parlor of a once-elegant mansion in Russell Street, Véronique de Bouvier huddled on a narrow bench fitted into the bow-fronted window. She was in her nightgown, a demure white cotton garment, ruffled and tied at the neck, the full sleeves covering her arms and hands except for the tips of her fingers. Her hair was hidden beneath a frilly cap of starched muslin.

Cotton and muslin, when she wanted to wear satin and silk.

A clock struck two. Véronique did not move. Many a night, when she was angry or sad, or merely restless, she sat in the window until the nearby Covent Garden Market came to life and the racket drove her to seek the relative quiet of her chamber at the rear of the ground floor.

The ground floor. She hated being confined to just one part of the house. It had not always been thus. At one time, she had a bedchamber and adjoining sitting room on the second floor, and the lower rooms were used for entertaining. But now, they no longer entertained. Every room of every floor but the ground level was let. Her home had become a lodging house.

Véronique did not often allow herself to dwell on

the past. Memories of past comforts tended to cast her into the dismals. She rather dreamed of the future, of gathering a little nest egg. She dreamed of love and marriage. Such dreams uplifted the spirits.

But not this night. And not ever again.

A by now familiar pain exploded in her chest. Gasping for breath, she sat up straighter, leaning her head against the cool window glass. Until that moment in St. Martin's Lane when Lord Northrop confirmed Peter's death, she had not known that pain caused by loss could be as sharply physical as pain caused by injury.

She had lost much—grandparents and an uncle to the guillotine, her country, the family fortune— but nothing had hurt as much as did the loss of Peter.

Oh, she knew the dream of love had been hers alone. For the present. She was convinced that, in time, after the marriage, Peter would have learned to love her. Only now, there was no time and there could be no marriage. Peter was dead.

She stiffened. Outside, in front of the house, a shadow moved, a shape darker than the night. The shadow turned into a man climbing the front steps. She heard the grating of a key in the lock.

Louis! Why was he back already?

He came straight into the parlor.

"Véronique?" he said softly into the dark.

She considered not answering. But he would return if he did not find her in her room.

"I am here." She did not attempt to speak French. To speak English was a principle with Louis. He conversed in their native language only with her parents and at *émigré* gatherings.

He shut the door and came toward the window.

A thud followed by an imprecation told her he had knocked against a piece of furniture.

"The deuce, Véronique! I wish you would rid yourself of this damnable habit of mooning about in the dark."

She rose and without a word lit the lamp on a small, round table in the window embrasure.

"What is the matter?" Louis gazed at her intently. "Are you not glad to see me?"

Her throat was so tight she could hardly speak. "You have not heard? About Peter?"

Something flickered in his eyes.

"What about him?" He tossed riding gauntlets and hat onto a chair. "I have heard nothing. I just rode in. Surely he did not make good his threat to return to active duty."

Her composure broke.

"He is dead!" she screamed. "Dead! Dead!"

Louis stared at her, his gaze hard, searching. "What do you know about his death? How did he die?"

"Is that all you can say? I tell you that Peter is dead, and you ask only how—"

Again, that awful, searing pain in her chest made her gasp for breath. Instantly, Louis was at her side.

"*Ah, ma petite. Ma pauvre petite,*" he murmured, wrapping his arms around her. "I am so very sorry. Do I not know how you feel about him? *Non?*"

The tears she had fought all day for the sake of her parents, who had no notion that she even knew an impecunious English naval lieutenant named Peter Marston, refused to be held back any longer. But it did not matter now that she gave way to emotion. Louis understood. He was once again the loving cousin, the older brother of her childhood days who had shared her sorrows as well as her joys.

She stood thus for a long time, her hands clutching the sleeves of his riding coat, her face buried against his chest, and her tears, no doubt, soaking him to the skin. Gradually, as she grew calmer, she realized that his words of consolation, although spoken in the tongue she loved above all others, were as mechanical as the awkward little pats on her back.

She raised her face and caught Louis looking at her strangely. There was pity in his eyes, but also impatience.

The childhood days were over. Forever. She and Louis would always be tied by the bonds of blood, of family. But the closeness was no longer there.

He did not hold her when she stepped away from him.

Straightening her cap, she said, "You wanted to know how Peter died. He was stabbed, I was told. Stabbed by footpads."

"Footpads?" Louis sounded incredulous. "Who told you?"

"Andrew Payne."

His eyes narrowed. "When did you see him? You had best tell me everything you know."

She moved away from the bow window and sat in a chair where her face did not catch the lamplight.

Tell Louis about the call on Miss Bancroft and the foolish tale she had invented for Lord Northrop's betrothed to justify a visit to Peter's lodgings? Tell Louis about the gentlemen from Whitehall staring at her when she arrived in St. Martin's Lane?

She had believed herself so clever, and then—

Non! She could not tell Louis of her foolishness.

"Speak, Véronique. I do not have much time."

She tapped a foot to mask the tension coiling in her. Why did she have the feeling that Louis knew more than he let on? She lost her slipper but did not bother to retrieve it.

"What happened in Rye, Louis? You were not expected back until tomorrow night."

He looked disconcerted by the change of topic. "Our man is dead. Drowned. Washed ashore two days ago."

"Another death."

"That is not the worst. The fool of a fisherman who found him also found the packet sewn into his coat."

Louis stepped closer. "Enough of the Rye business. I want to hear everything Andrew Payne told you about Peter. Everything."

The following morning, Friday, July fifth, Sophy went down to breakfast armed with notations on the deaths of Peter Marston and his servant. She might have saved herself the trouble, the hours of lost sleep it had cost to compile the list of copious theories and scanty facts as gleaned from Sir Jermyn, Andrew, and Lucian. There was no one with whom to discuss the matter.

Andrew, apparently, had spent the night at his chambers in York Street. And his lordship, she was informed by the footman when he brought her tea, was closeted in his study and had left orders not to be disturbed—unless news reached town that Napoleon's army had invaded the Channel coast.

Briefly, Sophy was diverted by a letter lying beside

her place setting. Lucian paid for early delivery of the post, but it was unusual that she was the recipient of a letter. Both her sisters—Linnet, who was nineteen, a junior mistress at a girls' academy in Bath; and Caroline, sixteen, still at Rose Manor but waiting to enter the Bath academy—tended to write only when they found themselves in some kind of bumble broth.

It was Linnet who had written. Not that she was precisely in trouble, but she informed Sophy she was leaving Miss Adbury's Select Academy two months earlier than planned. Her services in looking after the younger girls who could not go home for the summer were no longer required, since the new English and French mistress had arrived in Bath.

Sipping her tea, Sophy scanned the rest of the letter. She learned that Linnet would spend a few weeks with Caroline at Rose Manor. Then, if Sophy did not mind, she would come to London to stay at Payne House until Lady Sybil and Lord Makepiece returned from Scotland and she could assume her post as companion to Lady Sybil.

Mind?

Months ago, Sophy had begged Linnet to come to London. Lucian had added his entreaties to hers and offered his home and Miss Addie's chaperonage. He presented to Linnet the advantages of a Season in town, but she stoutly maintained she did not need a Season since she wasn't on the catch for a husband—a typical Linnet expression, which made Lucian say that he wouldn't have any trouble getting along with his future sister-in-law, since she was just as outspoken and stubborn as his beloved Sophy.

Lucian's beloved smiled mischievously as she refolded the letter and set it aside. Stubborn, was she? In that case, what could she do but prove him correct?

She spread out her notes on the murders.

Naval Lieutenant Peter Marston was killed on Wednesday, the night of the Dolwyn ball, between ten o'clock, when he left Andrew's chambers, and a quarter to eleven, when Horace found the body.

The death was reported to Andrew at Payne House about eleven-thirty, and Andrew informed the gentlemen from the Admiralty in Lord Dolwyn's study around midnight.

By two o'clock Thursday morning, Admiralty officials had searched Peter Marston's rooms in the presence of Peter's servant. The elderly man, who had originally been a groom in the employ of Marston's father, insisted when questioned that his master had not returned to the lodging house after he left for the Admiralty early Wednesday morning.

Question: where was Peter Marston between six o'clock Wednesday evening, when he left the Admiralty, and shortly before ten o'clock, when he asked Horace to let him into Andrew's study?

At eight o'clock on Thursday morning, on orders from the First Lord of Admiralty, Horace had gone to St. Martin's Lane to conduct a second, more thorough search of Peter Marston's rooms.

Horace found Peter's servant dead, the rooms in utter chaos. He returned to the Admiralty and was reporting to Lord Barham, in conference with the Marquis of Dolwyn, the Foreign Secretary, and Lucian, just as Andrew and Sir Jermyn Leister arrived.

The gentlemen repaired to St. Martin's Lane,

where, a short while later, Sophy arrived with Véronique de Bouvier.

Véronique . . . who had told Sophy she had an urgent note from Louis to Peter. A note that might contain information from France.

Véronique . . . who, apparently, lied as smoothly and easily as she captured the hearts of susceptible young gentlemen.

Poor Andrew. When he escorted Véronique home, she told him that she and Peter Marston had planned to wed in the autumn. There had not been a formal betrothal, but a date had been set in late October.

Question: which, if any, of Mademoiselle de Bouvier's confidences contained a grain of truth?

This was the part Sophy would discover. Lucian did not wish her to become involved with French agents and spies. She would honor his wish—even though she considered his philosophy that females should stay out of danger antiquated and quite stuffy.

She refused, however, to be totally banished from the investigation. Peter Marston had been a friend. She'd help find his murderer. And she'd start by questioning Véronique, who had made her believe they could become friends.

Eight

Sophy went into action at once. Skeet, the young boy Miss Addie had rescued from the streets, was sent to ferret out Mademoiselle de Bouvier's direction, while Sophy dashed off a reply to Linnet. She urged her sister to come to town as soon as possible and to bring Caroline and even Susannah, the wife of their guardian, who surely could use a holiday from her despotic spouse.

Sophy was sealing the letter when Skeet rushed into the parlor. His sharp, fox-like features glowed with pride.

"It's Russell Street, Miss Sophy. Near Covent Garden. Coachman drove Mr. Andrew once. He don't recollect the number off-hand, but he says if you want to go there, he would reckernize the house."

"Thank you, Skeet. But you should say he doesn't recollect," Sophy corrected automatically. "And he would *recognize* the house."

"Aye, Miss Sophy." Skeet shifted restlessly on legs that were as spindly after eighteen months of proper feeding as they had been the day Miss Addie saved him from a charge of pickpocketing. "Miss Sophy, why must I wait till the end of summer afore—before you can teach me again? I don't want a holiday!"

Sophy gave him a considering look. On Lucian's suggestion, she taught Skeet as well as Lucian's niece and nephews. When the children and their nurse left for the country, Miss Addie had decided that Skeet must have a holiday, too. The decision was prompted by kindness and generosity—but had it been wise? Daily, the butler received complaints about Skeet. Complaints from the kitchens, from the stables in the mews, even from the neighboring houses, that the boy was underfoot and getting into mischief.

"I'll speak to Miss Addie," she promised. "In the meantime, would you like to help me in an investigation?"

He flushed with pleasure and pride. "Cor, Miss Sophy! A real investigation? Like when you was—were after old Callums's murderer?"

"It does concern a murder. Two murders, in fact. But," she added truthfully, "only quite indirectly."

She rose from the desk, feeling just as disappointed as Skeet looked. She tousled his hair. "Cheer up. You never can tell what surprises will turn up in an investigation."

He brightened. "Shall I order the carriage, then?"

"Do that. And, Skeet!" she called after his retreating form. "You had also better let Miss Addie know that you're going out with me."

Sophy deposited her letter on the hall table for posting before going upstairs. A few moments later, properly attired in hat and gloves, she stopped on the first floor landing.

To her right, at the end of the corridor, was Lucian's study. The door was closed. He would not be pleased if she interrupted him with endless questions about the murder investigation. But if she were to pop in and wish him a good morning?

A blush warmed her face as she thought of his arms closing around her, his kiss, the caress in his voice. She started toward the closed door and was halfway down the corridor before it occurred to her that Lucian just might ask her plans for the morning.

Dash it! Her plans were innocuous enough. A visit to a young lady. However, the young lady lived in a neighborhood that might have been fashionable during the early part of the previous century but could now only be called questionable if not downright unsavory. And Lucian probably knew exactly where Mademoiselle de Bouvier lived.

Sophy did not doubt that he would insist she postpone the visit until he could accompany her. But Sophy did not want to wait. And neither did she want a companion during her talk with Véronique.

Slowly, reluctantly, she turned her back on the study. She wouldn't hesitate to use subterfuge when dealing with a suspect, but she would not lie to Lucian.

Skeet was waiting for her in the hall, or, rather, he was playing hopscotch on the marble tiles.

"Carriage will be along any minute, Miss Sophy." He traced an intricate pattern of hops and skips within the imaginary figure on the tiles. "I told Mr. Trueblood not to dawdle 'cause we're in a hurry."

"I'm sure he was impressed," Sophy said dryly.

She remembered Samuel Trueblood's imperturbability when Lucian had bundled her, protesting, into the carriage in St. Martin's Lane and ordered Samuel to drive her home. *Fast!* Unhurried, the coachman had climbed on the box. "I was drivin' Paynes and their ladies when you was still in short coats, my lord," he said from his perch. "An' you'll allow me to know what pace to drive in town so that it's safe for t'horses an' carriage. An' for Miss Sophy, too."

But if Samuel was irked by the page's admonition to hurry, he also had his pride to consider. And he prided himself on getting a team harnessed and the carriage out of the mews within a few minutes. He arrived at the door before Skeet had time to complete another round of his game.

Snatching up the pencil stub he had used for a marker, Skeet hurtled outside. "Come along, Miss Sophy! Mustn't keep the horses standing."

There was no danger of that. Sophy was as keen to get to Russell Street as he. A brief delay, however, was caused by Samuel Trueblood, addressing her from the box.

"An' does his lordship know where you're goin', Miss Sophy?"

One foot on the carriage step, Sophy looked at the groom holding the door, then at the coachman.

"Samuel, don't tell me you have orders to keep his lordship apprised of my movements!"

"Nay. But I'm tempted, Miss Sophy. Mighty tempted. Russell Street ain't no place for a lady."

She did not try to hide her relief, or her amusement at Samuel's attitude. Eyes dancing, she addressed the groom, a sturdy lad who had several times accompanied her on a ride in the park.

"Is that why you are going along, Mel? Gracious! I feel as if I had suggested a drive across some lonely heath."

"Not ter worry, miss." Mel lowered his voice. "It's

just that Mr. Trueblood is like a mother hen with an only chick. A bit of frolicking goes on around Covent Garden, but no harm intended."

As she joined Skeet in the carriage, she heard Samuel muttering darkly about lordships who leave orders not to be disturbed when they ought to know better. Hadn't Miss Sophy made it clear in St. Martin's Lane she was none too happy about getting separated from that French mamzelle?

Sophy chuckled but, quite properly, ignored Skeet when he wanted to know what was funny.

During the drive, she explained what she wished him to do while she talked with Mademoiselle de Bouvier. Skeet listened attentively, his eyes glowing, and his ears, those big saucers of ears that stuck out from his head like the arms on a signpost, turning red with excitement.

"Cor, Miss Sophy!" he said when she had finished and asked if he could do it. "Easy as eating pie! I just pretend I'm a Bow Street Runner. It'll be a lark, but I wish I had a notebook like that Runner that came to the house when Callums got herself murdered. An Occurrence Book."

"I'll give you a tablet of paper later on. But you mustn't write anything down while you're asking questions. Just think how conspicuous that would be."

"Conspicuous," he repeated, thrilled as always to learn a new word.

The noise and bustle of Covent Garden Market caught his attention, and he kept his face pressed to the carriage window until they crossed Bow Street.

"Miss Sophy," he said as the coachman reined in and stopped the carriage in front of the second house from the corner, "I'll not pretend to be a Runner after all. I'll pretend to be looking for a new post for my sister, who's a smashing good lady's maid and wants to work nearer our old mum, who's bedridden."

"Excellent. But, then, I always knew you had a quick mind." Sophy smiled at him but couldn't help wondering if he had hit upon the notion because he wished he truly had a mother and a sister.

Mel opened the door and let down the steps. Dismayed, Sophy stared at the filth-strewn pavement.

"This be the house I took Mr. Andrew," Samuel said from the box. "Mamzelle de Bouvier's house."

"Thank you." Sophy gingerly stepped down. "Samuel, I'm sending Skeet on an errand, and you, no doubt, will want to walk the horses. You may call for me in thirty minutes."

Skeet had already run off, disappearing beneath a dirty yellow sign with the faint lettering "Fishmonger."

Samuel shook his head. "I'll be stoppin' at the door every ten minutes. And Mel will wait right here."

Sophy could find no fault with the scheme. She looked up at the building. Three stories tall and with a wide, porticoed entrance, it was imposing enough to fit into any one of the elegant streets and squares of Mayfair. But there was a dull, tired look about it, an air of neglect and imminent decay.

Her father had money deposited in England when they fled France, Véronique had said. . . .

Holding her skirts high, Sophy approached the house and mounted the steps. She lifted the tarnished brass knocker, letting it fall against the equally tarnished plate.

It seemed an eternity before the door was opened—by Véronique herself. She was pale and turned even paler when she saw Sophy.

"Miss Bancroft! You should not—this is not a part of town you should visit."

"Don't worry about me." Sophy stepped past the young Frenchwoman. "I have a carriage, and a coachman and groom to lend me consequence."

Their eyes met; Véronique's fell. Without further ado, she opened a door immediately on her right. "Please come in, Miss Bancroft."

"Why don't you call me Sophy? You said yourself that we could easily become friends."

Véronique motioned to a chair. "That was before I knew of Peter's death."

Ignoring the chair, Sophy went to sit in the bow-fronted window overlooking Russell Street. She noted the worn chintz on the bench cushions, the threadbare rugs on the floor.

She looked at Véronique. "And what does Peter Marston's murder have to do with our friendship?"

Véronique encountered a clear, steady gaze from wide blue-gray eyes, and her heart sank. The previous night, she had acknowledged that it had been foolish to involve Lord Northrop's betrothed in her affairs. But until this moment she had not realized just *how* foolish. Miss Bancroft was not merely the "delightful if eccentric young lady" the *ton* had dubbed her. She was a power to be reckoned with.

Reminding herself that she had always enjoyed a challenge, she sat on the window bench opposite Sophy. "Mr. Payne told you that Peter and I were to be married in October?"

"I am sorry you lost your betrothed." Sophy would neither admit nor deny what she had learned from

Andrew or Lucian. She had come to Russell Street to ask questions, not to answer them. "And I regret very much that you had to hear of your loss in such a cruel manner."

"That was my own fault, was it not?" Véronique decided on a strategy. Frankness. She'd be as frank and open as she dared. She forced a smile. "If I had told you the truth about Peter and me, you would have broken the news more gently."

"Why did you lie, Véronique? Why, if you merely needed a chaperone to accompany you to your betrothed's lodgings, did you make up a preposterous tale about carrying an urgent message?"

"I did want to leave Peter a message. Mine. He promised to meet me at the Dolwyn ball. And when he did not, I started to worry. Peter had never broken a promise before."

"And he did not that night either."

"No." Véronique's voice shook. "He was already dead while I laughed and danced and waited for him."

Sophy pulled off her gloves, smoothing them carefully. She laid them atop her reticule.

"Still, you need not have lied to me, Véronique."

"I know that now. But when you asked if you were accompanying me to an assignation, I believed that only an intrigue would keep you interested in my errand."

"What a strange notion you have of me."

"Mr. Payne, he always said that you thrive on mystery and intrigue."

"Andrew talks too much!"

"Perhaps," said Véronique.

Unfortunately, Andrew Payne did not talk about the topics that mattered. And that was why she had schemed to improve her acquaintance with Miss Sophia Bancroft.

"If you wished to pique my interest with intrigue, why did you not tell me about your engagement to Peter?" asked Sophy. "It was a secret betrothal, wasn't it? A true romantic intrigue."

"Yes, it was a secret." Véronique folded her hands in her lap to stop them from trembling. "Only Louis knew. Peter and I took pains to appear mere acquaintances, because my parents consider me pledged to the Vicomte Marchand. We felt it would be best to say nothing until we could be married."

"And you could not marry immediately?"

"Peter wanted to wait. You see, in October, on his twenty-fifth birthday, he was to receive a sum of money, an inheritance."

Sophy felt strangely deflated. She had wanted to discover the true purpose behind Véronique's visit to Peter Marston's lodgings. She had learned the truth. At least, she didn't think Véronique was telling lies. And yet she felt dissatisfied with what she had learned.

"Lucian and I are waiting for my birthday," she said absently. "There won't be an inheritance, but I will no longer need my cousin's consent."

A carriage drew up in front of the house. True to his word, Samuel had returned after ten minutes. Skeet came running from a house across the street, exchanged a few words with Samuel and Mel, then went haring off in the direction of Covent Garden Market.

"Your carriage?" Véronique leaned closer to the window. "And Miss Addie's little page? You should have brought him in with you."

"Skeet likes to roam. He'll be happier exploring the market than sitting still inside."

Outside, Samuel Trueblood tugged at the reins. Slowly, the carriage started to roll.

"Sophy? Is there anything you can tell me about Peter's death? Anything about the . . . murderer?"

She sensed a change in Véronique. Tension so tangible it might have been a snake coiled between them.

She kept her gaze on the street. "Andrew told you, didn't he, that Peter was stabbed by a footpad?"

"Yes, he told me. But is it true?"

Sophy faced the young Frenchwoman.

"Why do you doubt it? What do you know, Véronique?"

Nine

"I know nothing at all." There was a harsh note in Véronique's voice. Her hands clenched in her lap. "But I have eyes to see and ears to hear. And I saw the Whitehall gentlemen at Peter's lodgings and heard you say to Lord Northrop that the rooms had been searched."

"Véronique, you accused the government—England's government—of killing Peter. Is that what you truly believe?"

"But that is foolish!" Bright spots of red burned on Véronique's pale skin. "I never said such a thing. Never! Or, if I did, I was confused."

Sophy kept her skepticism to herself, and after a moment, the flush faded from Véronique's face.

"But I ask myself," she said more calmly, "if you were correct, Sophy—if the Whitehall gentlemen did, indeed, search Peter's rooms—why would they do so when he was stabbed in a robbery?"

"They may have been looking for papers he took home to work on. After all, Peter was Lord Barham's aide."

They measured each other—Véronique intent, alert; Sophy guarded.

Sophy had accepted the Frenchwoman's earlier explanations. Everything Véronique said had held the ring of truth. Suddenly, the situation was changed. They were fencing with each other. And both knew it.

Véronique dropped her gaze. "Forgive me. I am not good company today. I did not sleep well, and I cannot think properly."

All very plausible—and yet, Sophy had trouble believing a word. Véronique seemed able to think very well, indeed.

Rising, Sophy gathered gloves and reticule. "I'll leave as soon as the carriage comes around again in a few minutes. But tell me. Do you still feel we can become friends?"

Véronique did not reply immediately.

"I do not know," she said finally. "To me, it all depends on why Peter died. But you—" She also rose, shrugging in a typically Gallic manner. "About you and how you will feel, I do not know, Sophy."

In the silence following Véronique's words, the slight squeak of the opening parlor door acted like a high-pitched scream. Sophy gave a start, and Véronique, turning the color of ivory, spun around.

The young ladies faced Louis de Bouvier, looking no less startled than they.

Louis recovered first. Smiling, he advanced on Sophy to bow gracefully over her hand.

"Miss Bancroft, I apologize for bursting in. I had no notion that Véronique had a visitor."

"I'm about to leave." Sophy had to tilt her head to meet his eyes, for he was tall. As tall as Andrew and Kit. "But you, monsieur—I believed you to be out of town."

"I was fortunate to be able to return sooner than I anticipated."

"Fortunate?" murmured Véronique. "It means you may have to leave again, does it not?"

The tension Sophy had felt earlier between her and Véronique now crackled between the cousins. But Louis, after one quick, hard look, ignored Véronique.

"Miss Bancroft, perhaps you will not mind telling Mr. Payne that, after all, I shall be able to accompany him to Tattersall's?"

"I do not mind a bit. The problem is, I may not see Andrew. I never know from one day to the next whether he plans to stop at Payne House or whether he'll go straight from the Admiralty to his chambers."

"But, of course!" De Bouvier put a hand to his brow, a hand that shook, and briefly covered his eyes. "Under the circumstances Andrew will want to be in York Street. So much closer to the Admiralty than Payne House! I do not understand how I could have forgotten even for an instant."

"What circumstances, monsieur?" Sophy asked cautiously. "What did you forget?"

"Peter," he said, his voice unsteady. "My poor friend Peter Marston."

Sophy was rendered acutely uncomfortable by the display of distress. Perhaps a Frenchman did not believe in a stiff upper lip. Perhaps a Frenchman was not taught that it was bad *ton* to show so much emotion.

Where was the carriage? She was certain that more than ten minutes had passed since Samuel had stopped. But when the sound of wheels drew her gaze to the window, she saw only a hackney and a carrier's cart.

Wanting to put distance between her and the

emotional Frenchman, yet not daring to leave the window embrasure with its view of the street, she said, "I know Peter's death must have been a shock to you. But why—"

"A terrible blow." De Bouvier visibly pulled himself together. "And what a tragedy for poor Véronique!"

Sophy glanced at Véronique, who stared at the tips of her slippers.

"Monsieur." Facing Louis again, Sophy doggedly finished the thought he had interrupted. "Why do you say that Andrew will stay close to the Admiralty because of Peter's murder?"

"Did I say that?" A curious light showed in de Bouvier's dark eyes. "And you, Miss Bancroft, are you saying my good friend's death had nothing to do with the fact that he was aide to the First Lord of Admiralty?"

If there had been something solid nearby to hold onto, Sophy would have snatched at it. First Véronique, now Louis, raised questions about Peter Marston's death. She felt as if someone were trying to pull the threadbare rug from under her feet.

She met his gaze boldly. "Lieutenant Marston, as I understand it, was attacked by a footpad."

"So I have heard. Forgive me, Miss Bancroft, but I do not believe it."

The rug had been pulled. Sophy searched for words that would, without giving away her knowledge of the matter, encourage de Bouvier to speak.

Véronique forestalled her, asking Louis almost the same question Sophy had asked her just a short while earlier.

"Why, Louis? Why do you not believe it?"

Her voice was hardly more than a whisper, yet on

Louis de Bouvier it had a startling effect. He looked at Véronique as if he had forgotten her presence. His mouth tightened to a thin white line.

With an obvious effort to appear calm, he said, "I know you do not share my concern about Bona-parte's agents roaming unchallenged in town. But you must admit that the death of a man connected with the Admiralty is suspicious in these uncertain times."

"Highly suspicious," Véronique said tonelessly.

Holding her breath as she looked from one to the other, Sophy noted the sheen of perspiration on Louis's upper lip, and—a startling contrast to her soft voice—the dangerous glint in Véronique's eye.

"Especially," said Louis, still calm but betraying some agitation in a more pronounced accent, "when the murdered man was on the brink of de-parture for one of the naval yards."

Véronique's dark eyes widened. "But I did not know."

Sophy heard the rattle of carriage wheels on the cobbles. This time, it was indeed Samuel, and he stopped squarely in front of the house. Tightening her hold on gloves and reticule, Sophy wished him to the dickens. She had just realized what bothered her about Véronique's confidences. The message— *her own message, not Louis's*—she said she wanted to leave at Peter Marston's lodgings.

Louis *had* given Véronique a message for Peter. Sophy had heard it with her own ears. And yet, Louis had known that Peter was about to leave town.

"I did not know," Véronique repeated, her atten-

tion fixed on her cousin. "You never told me that
Peter planned to be gone."

Louis de Bouvier made no reply but stepped
close to the window and looked out.

"Your carriage, Miss Bancroft. We must not keep
you."

Sophy would have given much to be able to stay
and encourage the cousins to talk. Instinct told her
it would do no good; instinct even warned her to
hide her curiosity. For now. She would be better off
when she next saw Véronique. Alone.

"Good-bye, Véronique. Monsieur de Bouvier. If I
see Andrew, I shall certainly give him your message."

"Thank you, Miss Bancroft."

Véronique said nothing. She still stared at her
cousin.

Louis de Bouvier accompanied Sophy outside
and, waving the groom aside, personally handed
her into the carriage.

"Miss Bancroft, I very much appreciate your calling on Véronique. This is a time of the greatest
difficulty for her. She and poor Peter . . ."

"Yes, monsieur?" Sophy said encouragingly when
he did not go on. "You were saying?"

"My cousin, she must have told you about her . .
. connection with Peter?"

"Indeed. I feel for her. Such a tragic loss."

"Ah, you do understand! I knew I could count on
you and your generosity."

"I'm afraid I don't follow you."

"Forgive me. I do not express myself as clearly as
I should. I am speaking of Véronique. Of her distress. You will make allowances, will you not, when
she seems— How do you say? Muddled?"

"Yes, of course. But frankly monsieur, I don't think you need to fear for your cousin. She appears to be as levelheaded as ever."

"Good. Very good." Louis nodded, but, despite his smile, he did not seem as happy with Sophy's reply as he should have been.

She heard a commotion in the street, the sound of running feet, the horses snorting impatiently; Skeet, his voice shrill with excitement, babbling about sweetmeats and other delights he had sampled; Mel's and Samuel's deeper tones, admonishing the boy to hush and settle down.

Sophy did not take her eyes off Louis de Bouvier. Warning instinct or not, there was one question she could not resist asking.

"Monsieur, you said that Peter Marston was on the point of leaving town when he was killed. How can you be so certain of that?"

His eyes narrowed. "Ah! You believe that could be of significance, Miss Bancroft?"

What a nasty habit he had of countering a question with a question. She herself had been known to employ the tactic—when she wanted to be sneaky or hide something.

"I don't know what may or may not be significant, monsieur." She smiled disarmingly. "I know only that I am very curious."

Louis did not quite return her smile, but he relaxed.

"I had it from Peter himself. I met him in the early evening on the day of the Dolwyn ball. He was on the way to his lodgings. To pack his saddlebags, he told me, for he was off to Bournemouth."

* * *

Sophy could not wait to tell Lucian. She wanted to discuss and analyze what she had learned in Russell Street, and also the bits of information Skeet had picked up while talking to shopkeepers and neighbors.

But Lucian was not home. He had left almost immediately after her departure for Russell Street.

Excitement drained as a wave of disappointment washed over her. She felt dull, empty. Lucian was never home.

She tried not to mind. And when, at luncheon, Miss Addie said what a pity it was that Lucian was kept so busy at a time when Sophy was free of her duties to the children, she assured Lucian's aunt that she quite understood.

"Oh, I never doubted that," Miss Addie said equably. "I'm sure you are showing more patience and understanding than any man has the right to expect of his betrothed."

Pensive, Sophy toyed with her fork. Perhaps she was too patient. Too understanding. Like a complaisant wife—easily ignored and forgotten when the situation demanded it.

"I'm sure it's a relief to Lucian that he need not fear a tearful scene or a burst of temper from you," said Miss Addie, innocently fanning the spark of resentment kindling in Sophy's breast.

"I believed Lucian tied to his study for the day." Sophy tried to appear as understanding as Miss Addie believed her to be. "Did Lord Mulgrave send for him?"

"Oh, no. Lucian was writing to the poor exiled King of France. And when he was done, naturally, he wanted to take the letter straight to Lord Mulgrave, who had a courier waiting."

For a moment, Sophy said nothing. A footman could have carried the letter to the Foreign Office!

She caught a stray thought and, because she felt just a bit out of charity with her betrothed, spoke it aloud.

"Lucian is a Whig. If he writes diplomatic letters, he should, like Mr. Fox, write to the revolutionary government. Not to a king nobody seems to want, least of all the French people."

"But, my love. Have you forgotten? There isn't any revolutionary government in France. Only an emperor."

Sophy gave a choke of laughter. Dear Miss Addie. Usually rambling when she talked, she could be right on target when it mattered.

The gray mood dispelled, Sophy took a bite of strawberries and cream served for dessert. "What about Andrew? Is he in the house?"

"No, he isn't. I haven't seen Andrew since the Dolwyn ball." A frown creased Miss Addie's forehead. "And the curious thing is, no one seems to know where he is today."

"If he's not working upstairs, he must be in York Street or at the Admiralty."

"But he isn't, Sophy! Early morning, he was at Whitehall, but no one has seen him since. That strange man who looks like a pirate with the gold ring in his ear came looking for Andrew."

Sophy knew only one man with an earring: Horace, the former marine who was now an Admiralty messenger and also served as Andrew's gentleman's gentleman in York Street. And if Horace did not know where Andrew was, no one knew.

"Was Lucian still here when Horace arrived?"

"Oh, no. Lucian was gone almost an hour."

Something was wrong. Sophy felt it in her bones. With a regretful look at the remaining strawberries in the bowl, she pushed back her chair.

"I had better have Samuel take me to York Street. Or did Horace return to the Admiralty?"

"Neither, dear. You see, Horace had some kind of accident. At least, he said it was an accident. If you ask me, he looks like someone who was engaged in a mill, as Andrew would say."

Miss Addie calmly spooned the last strawberries onto her dessert plate.

Sophy, standing beside her chair, clutched the back for support. Something was wrong, indeed.

"Horace was in a fight?"

"Well, dear, he does have a black eye. And there is a bloody gash above his ear."

"But where is he now, Miss Addie?"

"Upstairs, in Andrew's study. There is a chaise longue. I told him to lie down, and I sent Mrs. Waring to tend—"

Sophy heard no more. She was out of the dining room and flying up the stairs to the first floor, where Andrew had a study immediately opposite Lucian's.

Horace of the Admiralty with a black eye and a bleeding gash. An accident? Or, in view of Peter Marston's violent death, something more sinister?

Ten

"I was attacked," Horace said decisively.

He was a large, burly man. His complexion must generally be called ruddy, but this day his face resembled a round of pale cheese.

"There was three of 'em, Miss Sophy. One with a club. 'Twas him that felled me."

"I am sorry, Horace. Still, I'd say you are a very lucky fellow."

Grimacing, he touched the bandage wound turban fashion around his head. With the gold loop dangling from his ear, he truly did look like a pirate—a sadly battered pirate.

"I s'pose it could've been worse."

Much worse. Sophy shuddered. He could have suffered the fate of Peter Marston and his servant.

She pulled her chair closer to the chaise longue where Horace sat, his head resting against a bank of cushions. He had been lying down when she entered Andrew's study but, ignoring her protest, had insisted on sitting up. He might not be of the gentry, he told her sternly, but he knew better than to sprawl with his feet up in the presence of a lady.

Keeping her gaze averted from the slab of raw beefsteak on his blackened eye, she asked, "Do you have any idea why you were attacked?"

"I've a fair notion of what went on in their nous-boxes. A very fair notion." His mouth tightened. "It just so happened that this time the snitch pointed out the wrong man. I wasn't carrying no papers."

"You think they were French agents after Admiralty documents?"

"I doubt I'd have come out of the fracas alive if they'd been three French agents. No, Miss Sophy. They was nothing but riffraff and no more French than you an' me. Heard 'em clear enough. But they were acting under orders, either from the traitor himself or from the Frenchman he sells his tips to. Those thugs were lookin' for something very sp'cific. And when they didn't find it, they run off."

"Where did the attack take place, Horace?"

"York Street. Right outside Mr. Andrew's chambers."

"Were you leaving Mr. Andrew's rooms? Or did you come from the Admiralty?"

"Investigatin' again, Miss Sophy?" Horace gave her a weak grin. "I r'member when you went after Mrs. Callums's murderer. His lordship was fair shaking in his boots. Worriting himself sick he was, that you might get hurt."

"But I did not get hurt. And in this case, I'm only collecting a few facts to jot down and discuss later on with Lord Northrop."

Horace gave her a shrewd look. "I'll wager my earring his lordship don't know what you're up to."

Sophy refused to feel guilty. If Lucian had been home, she would have told him that she planned to become just a bit more deeply involved in the investigation than he might wish.

"Don't be stuffy, Horace. What harm is there in telling me what happened?"

"None that I can see." He grimaced again. "But, then, I didn't see no harm neither in going to York Street to make sure Mr. Andrew didn't forget about his lunch while he was lookin' for a code in those dratted letters."

"What letters? And didn't you tell Miss Addie that Andrew was *not* in his chambers in York Street?"

"He wasn't. That's why I came here. But at the time I thought that's where he'd be. In York Street."

"Horace, I think you had better tell me everything from the beginning."

"Ain't much to tell. I was helpin' Mr. Ashby and the other clerks when first Lord Dolwyn comes out o' Lord Barham's office, and then Sir Jermyn Leister comes out with Mr. Andrew. Sir Jermyn's about to go off after Lord Dolwyn, but stops in the door and gives Mr. Andrew this package. The letters I was tellin' you about. And Mr. Andrew—"

"Wait, Horace. Am I correct, you and the clerks were in Lord Barham's outer office? The room where Lieutenant Marston used to work?"

"Aye. We was to go through everything with a fine-tooth comb. The night Lieutenant Marston got killed the men were in a hurry and searched only the safe and the lieutenant's desk for the orders he was supposed to take to Admiral Calder. But now we're checking if he hid them in a file or something."

"I understand. So, then, you saw Lord Dolwyn leave Lord Barham's office."

A grin made Horace look almost his old robust self. "He shoots out as if fired by a fourteen-pounder. Would've knocked down Mr. Ashby if he hadn't jumped aside. His lordship was in a stew about something. I could tell, 'cause he slammed the door to the corridor. And that's not like him."

"All right. So, Lord Dolwyn is gone. Then Sir Jermyn and Andrew come out of Lord Barham's office, and while they're still in the outer office, Sir Jermyn gives Andrew this package of mysterious letters. Did Sir Jermyn say anything?"

"Aye, that he did. Let me see if I can remember." Horace closed his one good eye in the effort.

"'Almost forgot,' says Sir Jermyn an' pulls the package from his pocket. And he tells Mr. Andrew it comes from the Home Office, who got it from the Revenue Office in Rye. Seems a patrol, or mayhap 'twas fishermen, found this drowned fellow who had the package sewn in his coat. Letters. 'In French,' says Sir Jermyn. 'On the surface, quite innocent.' And then he claps Mr. Andrew on the back an' says, 'See if you can find something, my boy.'"

"The letters are legible?"

"They was wrapped in oilcloth. Never got wet."

"So, Sir Jermyn gave the letters to Andrew to check for coded messages."

"Right. And Mr. Andrew tosses 'em to me with orders to carry 'em straight to York Street 'cause he wants to have a word first with the men investigatin' Lieutenant Marston's death. Sir Jermyn says not to waste time on the men. They're a bunch of blundering fools or they would've caught the murderer by now. An' he goes off, muttering something about wanting to catch up with Lord Dolwyn."

Looking exhausted, Horace rested his head against the cushions. Sophy rose and poured a generous measure of medicinal brandy, which Mrs. Waring had thoughtfully left on Andrew's desk.

"Better drink some of this." Handing Horace the glass, Sophy examined the bandage for fresh bloodstains. "How bad is the head wound, Horace? Has Mrs. Waring sent for a physician?"

"Don't need no quack to tend me. And so I told her." He sniffed the glass, then sipped appreciatively.

"I'm sure Mr. Andrew would want you to—"

"No, he wouldn't," Horace said firmly. "Mr. Andrew knows I acted barber-surgeon more than once in me seafarin' days. Don't fret, Miss Sophy. I've seen enough head injuries to know I don't have no concussion."

"Very well. Are you up to answering more questions?"

"I'm as stout as can be. You just go right ahead and ask."

Sophy resumed her seat. "Those letters Andrew gave you—do you believe they are what the attackers were after?"

"Course they was. Only, I didn't have them no more."

Sophy could not help but compare a conversation with Horace to one with Miss Addie. In either case, extracting information was like drawing teeth.

"Who, then, had the letters?"

"Mr. Andrew did."

"Lud! You just said he gave them to you."

"Aye, but when we was walking down the corridor to the foyer, Mr. Andrew changed his mind and told me to give 'em back. And if that ain't a joke on the snitch, I don't know what is."

Rendered momentarily speechless, Sophy rose and paced between the chaise longue at one end of the long, narrow room and the door at the other.

"If you're thinking what I'm thinking," said Horace, "one o' them clerks must be the traitor."

"Or Sir Jermyn Leister."

"Miss Sophy!"

Horace sat up. He started to shake his head, winced, and thought better of making any unwise movement.

"Miss Sophy, if I didn't know better I'd think you was going soft in the head. Sir Jermyn! A most hon'rable gentleman."

"You're right, of course." She came to a stop before him. "This Mr. Ashby you mentioned, is he the man who took over Peter Marston's position?"

"No one's filling the lieutenant's position yet. But Nolan Ashby sure would like to. He's a senior clerk an' ruled over the First Lord's office when old Commodore Sweeney was aide, 'cause the commodore was no good for anything without a clerk."

"He was moved to another office when Peter Marston took over, wasn't he?"

"Aye. Ashby got sent to Lord Dolwyn's office. And when Barham took over from Melville, he tried to get back into the First Lord's office."

"Horace," Sophy said pensively, "would you judge Mr. Ashby a vengeful man?"

Slowly, Horace sat up. He peeled the beefsteak off his blackened eye and wrapped it in a napkin.

He met her gaze squarely. "Nolan Ashby is a man who don't know how to smile. His disposition, if not 'xactly choleric, is irritable. But any o' the underclerks will tell ye he's as painstaking in his work as he's competent. And he's as closed as an oyster."

"In fact," Sophy said wryly, "he is a paragon."

"And *you* think that makes him a 'spicious character."

"You cannot expect me to rule him out."

"Miss Sophy, if Lord Barham was ter ask me to

pick the one man who cannot be the snitch, I'd have to pick Mr. Ashby. Next to Mr. Andrew, o' course. Ashby has been with the Admiralty more'n twenty years. He's got no taste for gamblin' like Mr. Rignor, who started clerkin' only a year ago. He don't fancy the ladies and dandified garb like Mr. Wandsworth. And neither has he got a growing fam'ly like Mr. Sanders. A man don't easily turn traitor, Miss Sophy. In my experience, it's always debts that drives him to it."

"And Mr. Ashby has none?"

"Wouldn't want to take me oath on it—don't know Ashby all *that* well. But he's got ambitions to be alderman or something. Wouldn't make sense if he was to spoil his chances by peddlin' information to the enemy. Would it?"

"It was only a thought, Horace."

"Like Sir Jermyn?"

"And Lord Dolwyn. He, too, must have known of the letters."

Horace spluttered something unintelligible, and Sophy quickly changed the subject. "Now, if only we knew where Mr. Andrew is."

"Aye, it's got me worried. He said he'd go to the York Street chambers. But he weren't there. I checked as soon as those thugs ran off an' I got me breath to climb the stairs."

"I'm sure he'll show up."

Sophy hoped she sounded convincing. Horace needed rest, not worry. In fact, he ought to be in bed. She started for the door to speak to the housekeeper, but a sudden thought stopped her— one of the bits of information Skeet had gleaned from the Russell Street shopkeepers about the de Bouvier family.

"Horace, I understand Louis de Bouvier has chambers in York Street. Do you know if he lives near Mr. Andrew?"

"Course I do. A proper gentleman's gentleman makes it his business to know his master's neighbors." Horace chuckled. "When the curtains aren't drawn, Mr. Andrew and Monsieur Louis can look across the street straight into the other's sitting room."

Sophy raised a brow. The sitting room in York Street was also Andrew's study. And there, at the desk beneath the window, Peter Marston had written a note to Andrew.

"But, naturally," she said, "a proper gentleman's gentleman draws the curtains every night."

"As soon as it's time to light the lamps, Miss Sophy."

Giving herself a mental shake, Sophy left. She was getting fanciful again.

Eleven

Where the dickens was Andrew?

After arranging Horace's transfer to one of the guest chambers, Sophy had gone into the garden. It was far too hot and sultry to sit outside, but she worried about Andrew and did not want Miss Addie to know. So she sat in the gazebo and fretted.

If only Lucian were home.

She couldn't help but worry. Andrew carried an oilcloth-wrapped package, the letters from France, which in all likelihood lay at the root of the attack on Horace. Her ever-fertile imagination, with a deplorable tendency toward the gruesome, conjured Andrew lying somewhere, battered and bleeding like Horace. Or stabbed like Peter Marston and his servant.

She shivered despite the afternoon heat. The air was heavy and still. Oppressive. Perhaps she shouldn't have come to the gazebo. Here, the murderer of Callums, Miss Addie's abigail, had tried to kill a second time. Wasn't it logical that her fears intensified in this environment? Yet she did not leave.

Swiping at a stray curl that insistently tickled her cheek, she looked out into the garden, peaceful and quiet in contrast to her thoughts. Lavender grew in boxes beneath the window arches from which the glass panes had been removed for the summer months. She breathed deeply, letting the sweet fragrance soothe her mind.

As she grew calmer, her fears diminished. Nothing had happened to Andrew. He would show up with a perfectly reasonable explanation—reasonable to *him*. At three-and-twenty, he had not reached the age when an illicit boxing match at the Fives Court could no longer draw him from his desk.

Or, perhaps, he'd come in with Lucian. He might have gone to the Foreign Office to show the letters to his brother. No one had thought to check there, but Lucian occasionally assisted Andrew in the decoding of French documents. Both spoke French as if it were their native tongue, since their maternal grandmother, a Parisienne, had insisted on a French nurse and a French tutor for the boys.

Abruptly, Sophy's mind skipped to Véronique. Andrew might have gone to Russell Street. He believed himself in love with the young Frenchwoman.

And Véronique? She had obviously been in love with Peter Marston. They had planned to get married—in October, when Peter would have come into an inheritance.

If they had not waited, Véronique would have known happiness before she lost her love . . . .

Sophy thought about her own wedding. She and Lucian were waiting, too. It wasn't the same situation as with Véronique and Peter, who, apparently, had needed the inheritance to set up house. But— how silly it seemed now!—while waiting for the day she'd come of age, she and Lucian squabbled about the wedding date.

They had both agreed not to marry on her birth-day. A wedding day should not be shared with any other anniversary date. But Sophy, being very fond of odd numbers, wanted to marry on the third day of September. Lucian said he liked even numbers and opted for the second. And, he had pointed out more than once, the second was a day sooner than the third.

Sophy did not consider the squabble an impediment to the marriage. Long before September, they would reach a compromise. But now she did not want to argue even in jest about the wedding date.

September was only two months off, but for Sophy the time stretched endlessly. Perhaps, by then, she and Lucian would be strangers to each other. She did not think there was another young lady in all of England who saw her betrothed as little as she. Surely, that must change after the wedding. Then, they'd have the nights at least.

The nights. Sophy fanned her flaming cheeks. Two months were a long time to wait.

Or . . . did they have to wait?

If Lucian procured a special license, would a vicar ask if she needed the consent of a guardian? She did not look like a girl just out of the school-room. And, if need be, she could make herself look several years older.

She turned the tantalizing notion over in her mind. Lucian, too, had suggested an earlier wedding, but he wanted her to go to Rose Manor to obtain Jonathan's permission. An ill-advised move. Since the day they met, the day her mother was buried, Jonathan had done his best to spoil anything that gave Sophy pleasure.

When they were children, Sophy had physically attacked him for misdeeds against her sisters. Jonathan, five years her senior, had fought back but usually came out the loser. As they grew older, the fights turned into verbal battles, with Jonathan still on the losing side.

Then Sophy's father died, and Jonathan inherited Rose Manor and the title Baron Wingfield. And, since the late Lord Wingfield had made no other provisions for his daughters, Sophy, Linnet, and Caroline became Jonathan's wards. Jonathan finally had the upper hand.

If it weren't for Susannah, Jonathan's wife . . .

The crunch of gravel drew her attention to the path leading to the house. It must be Lucian, returned from the Foreign Office. And, since she heard two sets of footsteps, Andrew must be with him.

But it was neither Lucian nor Andrew who rounded the rhododendron hedge. Sophy caught her breath. Following the second footman was Jonathan Bancroft, her cousin and guardian.

By the great Jehoshaphat! She had made him appear merely by thinking of him. What the dickens did he want? She dismissed a sudden fear that Caroline had fallen ill or injured herself. Jonathan would not bestir himself to carry news, good or bad. He'd have penned a note.

Outwardly calm, Sophy remained seated in the wicker chair opposite the gazebo entrance and watched her cousin approach with firm, determined steps. Her insides might twist and knot, but Jonathan would never know.

"Lord Wingfield to see you, Miss Sophy," announced the footman and withdrew promptly.

"Sit down, Jonathan." Sophy indicated a sturdy wooden seat, more suitable to his bulk than the dainty wicker furniture. "What brings you to town?"

"Need you ask?" Mopping his brow, he shot her a baleful look. "Your scandalous position in this house, of course."

"Your wits have gone awandering. My position is no more scandalous now than it was when Lucian asked your permission to marry me."

"Permission I never granted!"

"But neither did you forbid the announcement of our betrothal."

"A bad mistake. Dammit, Sophia! How was I to know Northrop would be so foolish to announce an engagement while you're governess in his house! Especially when I made it clear I don't approve of the match."

"The only reason you don't approve is Sir Archibald Greynogge," Sophy said irritably. "After two years of being told no, you still hope I'll marry the old lecher so he'll forget your debts."

Jonathan's fleshy countenance turned red. Not in shame; Sophy knew he had none. When Jonathan flushed, it was in anger.

"You're my ward, Sophia. I have the right to tell you what to do. I have the right to decide whom you may or may not marry."

Sophy fought the urge to jump up and pace. He must not know that he had the power to upset her.

"I have told you before, the only way you could have forced me to the altar with Sir Archibald is drugged, knocked senseless, or kicking and screaming all the way. And even at the altar, I would still say no."

"Yes, you'd set up a ruckus! I never doubted it."

His voice was tight with anger. "You have so little regard for our name, you'd plunge us all into scandal. You knew you could blackmail me into letting you hire yourself out as a governess! *A governess!* You, a Bancroft of Rose Manor!"

"I would have worked as a scullery maid rather than marry Sir Archibald."

"You think you've been so clever! Threatening to blacken my name—until I gave you permission to become a governess. Threatening me again, until I allowed you to have Linnet educated in Bath. And yet again, until I let you enroll Caroline for the next term."

"Because you dismissed *our* governess."

"Bah! Girls don't need an education. They're meant to marry."

An old argument. Sophy had no intention of renewing it. Drawing a steadying breath, she leaned back in the chair.

"Since you know you cannot make me do your bidding, why have you come, Jonathan?"

"Because this time, you *will* listen to me."

He rose, his height and bulk intimidating. "This time, you have no threat to hold over me. This time, you'll obey. For it's you who'll suffer from the scandal if you don't do as I say."

"What the dickens are you talking about, Jonathan? There is no scandal."

"There wasn't while the children provided a legitimate excuse for your stay in Northrop's house. But the children have been gone over a month. You are compromising your honor by living here. You're besmirching our name!"

"Balderdash!"

He took a threatening step closer. "Pack your

bags, Sophia. You are coming home with me. Today."

"I most certainly will not."

"You have no choice. This time, you may kick and scream as much as you like. I shan't care who hears you. There isn't a family man in all of England who will not side with me. I am doing my duty. I am protecting my ward's honor."

"You are mad, Jonathan. Stark raving mad. My honor has never been called in question."

"I have it in your own writing that the children are not here, and that the old lady who is supposed to be your chaperone spends most of the day in her own rooms."

"You read my letters to Susannah!"

"Susannah is my wife. I have a perfect right to read her correspondence."

Sophy could sit still no longer. She jumped to her feet. Arms akimbo, she faced her cousin.

"You are a brute, Jonathan! Susannah would not have shown you a letter from me if you had not bullied her."

"And you're a deceitful wretch! I forbade Susannah to correspond with you. But with your sly, insinuating manners, you encouraged her to go behind my back."

That was not true. Susannah had asked her to keep writing, but she'd bite off her tongue before she betrayed Susannah to her husband.

"I'm not here to discuss my wife." Jonathan's hand clamped around Sophy's upper arm. "Come along, miss. I have the carriage waiting at the door."

"Let go!"

Sophy smartly kicked his shin. The kick hurt her toes more than it did his booted leg, but Jonathan, remembering previous encounters, released her arm and took a prudent step backward.

"Baggage!" His face turned puce with fury. "Either you come with me or I'll have my groom carry you out to the carriage."

"You wouldn't dare! Lucian would call you out."

"My love." Unhurried, Lucian entered the gazebo. "I cannot possibly call out my future cousin-in-law."

She had instinctively started toward him, but now she stopped, standing between him and Jonathan.

"Why not? Jonathan is a *toad.*"

Lucian's mouth twitched. His Sophy. His delight. He shot a look at Sophy's guardian, who stared back belligerently but seemed disinclined to argue.

"Because, my love—" Lucian raised her hand to his lips for a lingering kiss. "Because it is bad *ton* to call out a cousin. And it is quite out of the question to challenge a toad."

She was neither amused nor appeased and indignantly removed her hand from his clasp.

"Did you hear what he said?" she demanded. "Did you hear what he plans to do?"

Lucian gave her a pensive look. When he left the study earlier that morning and asked his aunt where Sophy was, he had learned that she had ordered the carriage and taken Skeet with her on an errand. A question or two dropped casually in the stables brought to light her destination. Russell Street, where Mademoiselle de Bouvier lived.

"Lucian! Surely, you don't want me to go with Jonathan!"

"You have no choice," Jonathan reminded her. Lucian's sudden appearance had rendered him speechless, but he quickly recovered his aplomb.

"And neither does Northrop. You're under age, Sophia."

Seeing the light of battle in his beloved's eye, Lucian placed an arm around her waist. "Allow me to handle this."

"I know how to deal with Jonathan."

"My love, you've been on your own too long. You forget that now you have me to fight your battles."

Lucian did not wait for her reply but turned to Jonathan. "Come along, Wingfield. You must be tired after your journey. My aunt will see to it that a chamber is prepared for you."

Jonathan sputtered but found himself unable to resist the command in that quiet voice. He preceded Lucian from the gazebo.

Lucian smiled at his betrothed. "I'll be back."

"You're inviting him to stay?" she asked, incredulous.

"It is only polite."

"*Polite*? Lucian, it is outrageous! Don't you understand, he—"

"We shall talk presently. I promise, I'll be back. I'll merely present your cousin to Aunt Addie. She'll arrange everything that's necessary. Give him tea. Order a room prepared."

Sophy's breast swelled. "Well, don't have her put Jonathan into the yellow chamber. That's where I put Horace, who has a black eye and a nasty, horrid gash on his head."

For an instant, she believed she had succeeded in startling him. Then he bowed, as unperturbed as ever.

"I'll return as soon as I can."

Sophy looked after him as he accompanied Jonathan into the house. She hadn't really wanted him to call Jonathan out. Or had she? With resentment nagging at her, she couldn't be certain on that point.

But she did know she wasn't satisfied with Lucian's handling of Jonathan. Lucian had been too polite, too reticent. As if he were dealing with a sensitive foreign dignitary. And if that was what the diplomatic service did to a man, she wasn't sure she liked it.

Twelve

As they entered the house through the French doors of the morning room, Lucian placed a detaining hand on Jonathan's arm.

"Wingfield! A word of caution. I may not be able to call you out without creating a damned unpleasant stir, but I can and will draw your cork if you annoy Sophy."

"You've no right to interfere," Jonathan blustered. "I'm only doing my duty. You've sent the children into the country but kept Sophia here. She's compromised, and I've come to take her home."

"Noble sentiments, Wingfield. But if you believe Sophy compromised, why the devil don't you demand that I marry her immediately?"

"Don't want a Whig in the family. Bancrofts have always been Tories. Always will be."

"The Paynes are Tories, too. I'm the only black sheep in the family."

"Belong to the Prince of Wales's set, I don't doubt." Jonathan gave him a look in which derision fought with envy.

"Couldn't if I wanted to," Lucian said wryly, then grinned at the memory of his rare meetings with the Prince of Wales. "His Royal Highness considers me too stodgy for his set. He might welcome you with open arms, though. I believe you're fond of gambling?"

Jonathan colored angrily. He was disastrously fond of gaming. "Don't try to change the subject, Northrop. Sophia—"

"That subject is closed. Whether you like it or not, Sophy and I will marry with or without your consent as soon as she's of age. In the meantime, leave her alone, or you'll have me to reckon with."

Lucian crossed the room to usher the visitor into the entrance hall.

"Why don't you stay a few days, Wingfield? Accompany Sophy about town and satisfy yourself that there's no scandal whatsoever attached to her name. Or to mine, for that matter."

Jonathan hesitated. Stay in town? With no drain on his purse, except for what he needed at the clubs . . . White's . . . Brooks's. The stakes were more to his liking at Brooks's, but the place had become too Whiggish for his taste.

"Afraid to be convinced?" asked Lucian, who had his own reasons for wanting Sophy's cousin to stay. "Afraid you'll have to admit you were wrong? I assure you, the *ton* has proclaimed Sophy a delightful young lady. You should be proud of her."

"Delightful?" Jonathan gave a snort. "Don't see how anyone can call her other than a shrewish vixen."

"Then I wonder you aren't glad to get her off your hands."

Jonathan looked baffled, and without further ado, Lucian handed him over to a footman with orders to take the visitor to Miss Addie and to have the housekeeper prepare a chamber.

Heading back to the garden, Lucian hesitated before stepping through the French doors. Perhaps he should take a moment to find out what fracas Horace had been involved in to earn himself a black eye and a gash on the head.

But, no. Sophy came first. And besides, whatever he might learn from Horace, Sophy would be able to tell him. Without a doubt, she had persuaded the hapless man to give her the full story.

Sophy awaited Lucian's return with mixed emotions. If only Jonathan hadn't shown up. Not that he could intimidate her—but she wasn't at all happy about the effect his presence had on Lucian.

A few moments' contemplation had brought her to the conclusion that Lucian's courteous manner toward Jonathan was by design. Lucian had a scheme, and she suspected very much the scheme was to keep her out of the Admiralty investigation of Peter Marston's death.

But, surely, Lucian did not expect her to return to Rose Manor with Jonathan. Not two months before the wedding. Not when they hardly saw each other, even living in the same house.

She heard his step on the graveled path, his soft, melodious whistling.

"Well?" she asked as soon as he entered the gazebo. "Is Jonathan staying?"

Holding out both hands, Lucian went toward her. Firmly, he drew her out of the wicker chair. He might not know how to stop her from plunging headlong into a dangerous investigation, but he did know how to stop her from asking questions.

Enfolding her in his arms, he bent his head and kissed the lips that were about to form another "Well?" Her mouth opened to him. Her arms wound around his neck to draw him closer. He tasted sweetness, desire, promise.

No longer was stopping her questions a consideration. He could think only how much he loved her. How little time they'd had together since their betrothal. He wanted to go on kissing her and holding her forever.

But every kiss must come to an end. They stood locked in each other's arms and looked at each other.

"I love you, Sophy."

Her arms tightened. "I love you, Lucian."

"There's no doubt about it, my love. You *must* marry me."

"Now?" Her eyes sparkled. "A capital notion! Let's have a Fleet marriage."

He kissed her pert little nose. "I'd like nothing better. Alas, the Act of 1753—"

"I know." Her arms slipped from his neck. "It's too horrid. Even for a Fleet marriage a proper license is required. But, at least, a cleric imprisoned for debt won't ask too many questions."

Lucian grew thoughtful. "No questions about the bride's age or a guardian's consent."

"Lucian! I was jesting. Just think what a Fleet marriage would do for your career!"

He crushed her to his breast. There were times when he wished his career in the diplomatic service to the devil. He wondered if it truly would be a penance to retire to the country and oversee the estates, presently administered by two very competent stewards.

"But listen to me, Lucian." Her voice was muffled by the cloth of his coat. "I have decided that we shall no longer squabble about the wedding date. We'll get married on the second day of September."

"We will?" Seating himself on a cushioned bench, he drew her down beside him. His fingers played with the soft curls clustered on her neck. "Have I convinced you there's no magic in odd-numbered dates?"

She hesitated. "No."

He suppressed a smile. Her superstition rather delighted him, and his insistence on an even-numbered date was mostly a game. She was usually such a levelheaded, fact-conscious person that he hadn't been able to resist teasing her.

"Then, perhaps, you have come to the conclusion that the male partner has the greater right to choose the wedding date?"

She pokered up immediately. "Of course not!"

But her indignation was short-lived. She said softly, "It's what happened to Véronique and her wedding plans that made me realize how very silly, how frivolous our squabble was."

A weight settled on his shoulders. Véronique de Bouvier . . .

"Sophy, about Véronique—"

"I went to see her this morning, Lucian."

Sophy leaned against him. She spoke hurriedly, not wanting him to interrupt with a reproach or with questions.

"Véronique is upset, of course. But I think she is also a little frightened. She is hiding something, Lucian! I'm not saying she told outright lies, but she is keeping something back."

He allowed her to talk. It was better this way. Sophy would analyze the situation even while she reported it. Her intuition would do the rest, and she would recognize Mademoiselle de Bouvier for what she was.

"Lucian, she now says that it was her own note she wanted to leave for Peter. She was concerned because he had not shown up at the Dolwyn ball as promised. But I know for a fact that Louis gave her a message to be delivered to Peter."

Lucian had not believed it possible that anything Sophy had to report would startle him. But this did. A message from Louis de Bouvier to Peter Marston on the night Peter was killed, did not fit the picture at all.

"How do you know, Sophy?"

"I was there when Louis reminded Véronique. It was when he left Dolwyn House. He told her not to forget his messages. One for Andrew. One for Peter."

She tilted her head inquisitively. "Why does this make you frown?"

"I'll explain in a moment. First tell me what else you learned from Véronique."

"Not much more. Louis de Bouvier joined us— You're frowning again, Lucian! And if you don't stop playing with my hair, you'll give Jonathan an excuse to call me a loose woman."

"Jonathan be damned." Lucian moved his hand to her ear and tugged gently. "Just get on with your tale so I can ask you about Horace and his black eye."

She sat bolt upright. "Where's Andrew? I hoped he'd be with you."

"I daresay he'll be in later. He mentioned some

letters he must decode, but, at present, he is with the men investigating Peter's death. They're trying to find a witness to the stabbing."

"When did you see Andrew? Horace was worried. He thought Andrew would be in his chambers."

"Horace worried?" Lucian cocked a brow. "Or you?"

"It makes no odds," she said, her tone brisk. She truly must learn to curb her imagination. "Andrew should have left word."

"You and I might think so. But Andrew?" Lucian smiled. "He was in fine fettle when I encountered him on my way to Whitehall. He was with two of the Admiralty investigators. *Assisting* them, he said."

Sophy's eye kindled. Investigating was *her* forte. *She* should be assisting the Admiralty men.

"He'll make a mull of it, I don't doubt. Do you remember the utterly ridiculous suspicion he had when Callums—"

Lucian pressed a finger to her mouth. "I do, my love. Now, back to Louis de Bouvier. He joined you and Véronique. And?"

"Did you know that Peter told him he'd be going to Bournemouth?"

"No. De Bouvier admitted this?"

"He said Peter told him early the evening of the Dolwyn ball, which makes it particularly strange that later that night Louis gave Véronique a message for Peter."

"Let's forget the message for the moment. What else can you tell me about Louis or Véronique?"

"Mind you, this is just an observation, but I noticed a friction between the cousins as soon as Louis entered the parlor. I'm not a judge of their relationship since I don't know them intimately and hardly ever encountered them together, but the tension, almost antagonism, puzzled me. Everyone has always said they are devoted to each other. Like siblings."

"And they were at odds?"

"It was more as if they didn't quite trust each other."

"Go on."

"Lucian, did you know that Louis de Bouvier has chambers in York Street? Across from Andrew?"

"Yes, my little investigatrix. I knew."

She frowned at him. "Why are you looking at me like that?"

"Like what?"

"Not quite smiling. Not quite scowling. Just . . . resigned, I suppose."

"Because I know what your next question will be, my observant Sophy."

"Then," she said, her eyes widening, "my imagination is not running away with me when I suspect that Louis is one of the French agents he condemns at every opportunity?"

"Not at all."

She put a hand to her mouth as if to stifle an exclamation or to smother a question. He waited a moment, but she did not ask about Véronique, an omission he found disquieting.

"There was an incident in the fall of last year that brought Louis de Bouvier to the attention of an Admiralty agent," he said. "So it was arranged that Andrew, since he moves in the same circles as Louis, would take a set of rooms near de Bouvier."

Sophy's hand dropped. "And Andrew struck up a friendship with Louis."

"Actually, no. It was Véronique who introduced

Andrew to her cousin. And that was several months before the Admiralty decided to keep Louis under surveillance."

Sophy did not meet his eyes. "Do you believe Véronique is working with Louis?"

"What do you believe, Sophy?"

Thirteen

Sophy was silent for so long, Lucian did not think she would answer.

She looked up. "It is quite possible. But, dash it, Lucian! I like her!"

He was careful not to show dismay. If Sophy liked Véronique, he saw pitfalls ahead. It was more urgent than he had realized to distract her from the investigation of Peter's murder.

"Sophy, don't get too close to Mademoiselle de Bouvier. We don't know how deeply she's involved, but she is Louis's cousin. And Louis is top on the list of suspects for the death of Peter Marston."

If he thought he would startle her, he was disappointed.

She merely said, "I didn't see Louis de Bouvier at Dolwyn House until very late. I suppose it has been verified what time he arrived?"

"At midnight. Andrew met him in the foyer. Admiralty agents are trying to learn if Louis was in York Street between ten and eleven that night. But, you can imagine, it's a damnably slow process."

"Yes, you wouldn't want it to come to his ears," she said absently, trying to picture the elegant Frenchman lurking behind the curtains of his sitting room window while Peter Marston entered, then, a few minutes later, left Andrew's building.

"I wonder why Louis admitted he knew that Peter was about to leave for Bournemouth."

"It worries me that he did." Lucian took her hands and clasped them firmly. "It would worry me even more if I thought you planned another visit to Véronique."

"But Véronique has nothing to do with Peter's death. Great heavens, Lucian! She loved him. They were to be married this October."

"Were they? No one knew of an engagement. No one even knew that Peter's interest in Véronique ran deeper than that of the other dozen or so gentlemen of her court. In fact, I'd wager a pony that Andrew is more smitten than Peter Marston ever was."

"It was a secret engagement. Lucian, does Andrew think like you? That Véronique is Louis's accomplice?"

A shadow crossed his face. "No. Like you, he has trouble believing ill of her. Sophy, promise not to visit—"

"I promise to be careful when I see Véronique," she cut in. "Please don't ask more than that."

"Sophy, I cannot and will not permit you to involve yourself in a dangerous investigation. A half dozen or more Admiralty men are tracing Louis's movements that night. They are also investigating Véronique, and—"

"And a lot of good they've done so far!"

A weight settled on his shoulders as he looked into her mutinous face. He remembered their stormy courtship, the many times he had wanted to shake her.

But he also remembered that he had fallen in love with her, not *despite* the characteristics he'd been raised to consider faults, but *because* she was stubborn, impertinent, fiercely independent, and courageous to the point of foolhardiness.

"Lucian, I will not make a promise I cannot keep. If Louis, indeed, killed Peter, Véronique will need a—" Sophy hesitated, then said firmly, "A friend."

He wished he could tell Sophy she was talking nonsense. But that, he knew, was not one of her faults.

"Why?"

"Whether or not she was an accomplice in Louis's spying activities, she was *not* involved in Peter's death. She loved him. And if she begins to suspect her cousin—which, no doubt, she will, for she's not at all dull-witted—she may be in danger, too."

"I see your point." He tightened his grip on her hands. "But it only enforces my view that *you* will be in danger."

Her eyes flashed. He thought she would wrench away. Then, suddenly, her expression softened.

"Lucian, you worry too much. I know it is because you shouldered the responsibilities of head of the family at a very young age, but please remember that I am not your ward. I am your betrothed, soon to be your wife. I'd stifle if I let you have your will—which is to wrap me in cotton wool and keep me safely in a strongroom."

"Devil a bit! You make me sound an ogre."

She smiled. "Go ahead. Shake me. I know you want to. You always do when I exasperate you."

He crushed her to his breast. "Sophy, be care-

ful! And promise not to do anything or go anywhere without letting me know."

"That I promise."

He held her tightly. Was he a fool for letting her
have her way? No doubt, he was. But, if she were
meek and biddable, would he love her quite as
fiercely as he did?

Omitting the shaking, he kissed her until lack of
breath forced them to pull apart.

"Lucian, I love you."

"How do you think I feel? I love you to distraction."

He rose from the bench and started pacing the
tiled floor. If they could get married soon . . . tomorrow . . . today . . .

"What about Peter?" asked Sophy. "Whether the
story of the engagement is true or not, he seems
to have been more deeply involved with Louis and
Véronique than anyone knew. Is he above suspicion?"

Reluctantly, Lucian banished the dream of an immediate wedding night.

"He *was* above suspicion. Until Véronique accused our government of having killed him."

"Yes, it puzzled me."

"It was a very odd thing to say, even considering
that Véronique was distressed. But it makes sense if
Peter Marston was the traitor at the Admiralty."

"I don't want to believe it. But, I suppose," Sophy
said slowly, "if Véronique knew Peter passed information to Louis, she might jump to the conclusion
that Peter's activities had been discovered and he
was killed by an *English* agent."

"That is exactly the conclusion drawn by the gentlemen of the Board of Admiralty, with the exception of Lord Dolwyn and Sir Jermyn."

"And the First Lord? Does he believe his aide committed treason?"

"Barham was inclined to believe in Peter's integrity. But yesterday afternoon an Admiralty clerk stepped forward and reported having on two occasions seen Peter hand papers to Louis de Bouvier."

Sophy gave a sniff. "How very likely! And where did the observant clerk witness the transaction? Perhaps in the foyer of the Admiralty?"

"In the Brown Bear in Bow Street."

"You jest! That's the tavern where Bow Street Runners hobnob with criminals in order to pick up information. Lucian, the place is notorious! And even if Peter met Louis there, what was the clerk doing in that tavern? If I were Lord Barham, I wouldn't believe a word that man says."

"A great number of very respectable men, whose only vice is curiosity, frequent the Brown Bear precisely because it is a place where the law rubs elbows with pickpockets, house breakers, and bridle culls."

"Oh, yes?"

"Yes, indeed. Marcus Wandsworth, the clerk in question, is a very respectable and respected man and has served the Admiralty for more than thirty years."

Sophy frowned. Hadn't Horace mentioned Mr. Wandsworth?

"Are you certain, Lucian? I mean, about the man's respectability. Horace described a Mr. Wandsworth to me—a man with a penchant for ladies and a dandy's elegant clothes."

"That would be Simon Wandsworth, Marcus's son. He's a different kettle of fish. He's been with the Admiralty three or four years and is rather a disgrace. But, like you, the elder Mr. Wandsworth is interested in the detection of crime. He's a friend of the chief Bow Street Runner, and their meeting place is the Brown Bear."

"I don't suppose you can ask for a more respectable or reliable man than a friend of a Bow Street Runner."

Lucian cocked a brow. "Do I hear disappointment?"

"No." Sophy's look was rueful. "Reluctance to let go of a theory that could have applied to the disgraceful younger Wandsworth."

"In that case you had better tell me why Horace mentioned him to you and why he has a black eye. Did he come to blows with Simon Wandsworth?"

"If that were all! Horace was attacked because someone believed he carried letters found on a drowned man near Rye. The letters Andrew is supposed to decode."

"Dash it, Sophy! You might have told me sooner."

"It's your fault. I forgot about Horace when you kissed me. And then we started talking about Véronique and Louis."

"And I kissed you again."

"So you did," she said, looking her most demure. "Besides, the letters are safe with Andrew."

"Quite safe, since Andrew is escorted by two of the best Admiralty agents. But I'll have a word with Horace. Did you say he's in the yellow chamber?"

"Yes."

Lucian pulled her to her feet. "Come with me. As

long as I'm home for an afternoon, I want to make the most of your company."

Before Sophy could utter a word in reply, a young lady came hurtling down the gravel path.

"Sophy!" cried Lady Jane Hawthorne.

Breathless, her face as white as paper, she stumbled into the gazebo.

"Sophy, you must do something! They've arrested Andrew for the murder of Peter Marston."

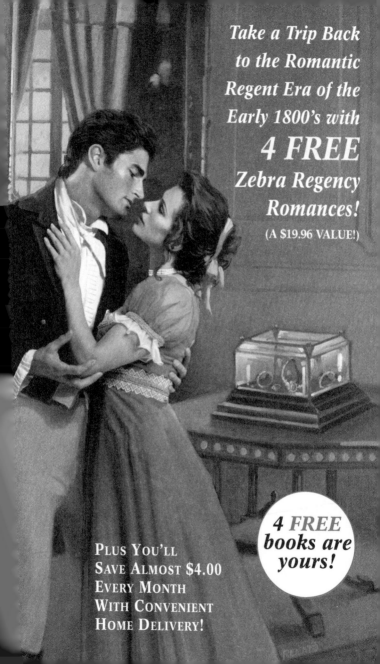

We'd Like to Invite You to Subscribe to Zebra's Regency Romance Book Club and Give You a Gift of 4 Free Books as Your Introduction! (Worth $19.96!)

If you're a Regency lover, imagine the joy of getting **4 FREE Zebra Regency Romances** and then the chance to have these lovely stories delivered to your home each month at the lowest price available! Well, that's our offer to you and here's how you benefit by becoming a Regency Romance subscriber:

- **4 FREE** Introductory Regency Romances are delivered to your doorstep (you only pay for shipping and handling)

- 4 BRAND NEW Regencies are then delivered each month (usually before they're available in bookstores)

- Subscribers save almost $4.00 every month

- You also receive a **FREE** monthly newsletter, which features author profiles, discounts, subscriber benefits, book previews and more

- No risks or obligations...in other words, you can cancel whenever you wish with no questions asked

Join the thousands of readers who enjoy the savings and convenience offered to Regency Romance subscribers. After your initial introductory shipment, you receive 4 brand-new Zebra Regency Romances each month to examine for 10 days. Then, if you decide to keep the books, you'll pay the preferred subscriber's price, plus shipping and handling.

It's a no-lose proposition, so return the FREE BOOK CERTIFICATE today!

ll..l..ll....lll...ll.l.l.l..l.l..ll.l.l..l.l..ll..ll...l

REGENCY ROMANCE BOOK CLUB
Zebra Home Subscription Service, Inc.
P.O. Box 5214
Clifton NJ 07015-5214

PLACE
STAMP
HERE

Fourteen

"Impossible!" said Sophy.

"What utter rot!" said Lucian, then, rather white about the mouth, apologized for his language and, without an explanation, strode off.

Frowning, Sophy watched him disappear. He did not go toward the house but toward the narrow gate set in the back of the garden wall—the gate that opened directly onto the mews and the stables.

Surely he did not, despite the vehement denial, believe Jane's nonsense?

In the sudden silence following the slam of the closing gate, Sophy was aware of the afternoon heat, a certain sultriness and stillness of air that presaged a storm.

"Let's go into the house." She placed an arm around Jane's waist. "You look as if you're about to swoon. You walked here, didn't you? Truly, you ought to know better in this heat."

Jane shook her off. Gone was the poised, mild-mannered young lady who had won the hearts of the *ton*. Instead, Sophy saw the little hoyden with the mussed hair and torn flounces Kit had talked about before Jane's appearance in town.

"What does it matter how I got here?" Jane looked perilously close to stomping a foot. "Andrew has been arrested! Why do you refuse to believe me?"

Unease stirred in Sophy. The girl sounded so urgent. So certain. And very frightened.

Sophy remembered the first encounter in April between Andrew and Jane, the catch in Jane's breath when they were introduced, the sudden blush that faded to an alarming paleness. Clearly, the girl had tumbled head over heels in love. But, then, she had seen Andrew with Mademoiselle de Bouvier and had hidden her feelings behind a charming social smile. Until now.

But Jane could not possibly be right. The thought of anyone suspecting Andrew of murder and arresting him was simply too ludicrous.

"Jane, it makes no sense," Sophy said gently. "Andrew is helping to *investigate* the murder. All morning, he was with the Admiralty men trying to find a witness. Somebody misunderstood the situation and stupidly started a nasty rumor."

"It's no rumor. Papa came home all in a pother. I heard him talking to Kit. They found the witness, Sophy! An ostler, who says he saw Andrew stab Peter Marston."

Sophy's breath caught. "The man lies!"

Her cry was drowned in a sudden rustle of leaves as a gust of wind swept through trees and shrubs. Clutching her billowing skirts, she grabbed Jane's hand and pulled her toward the nearest access to the house, the kitchen door.

The bright day turned dark. Raindrops, fat and heavy, pelted them, plastering the thin muslin of their gowns to their backs. Thunder rumbled in the distance. The storm had broken.

The kitchen was quiet and empty, but from the

servants' hall came the sound of voices, the scrape of cutlery against china. It was a quarter past three o'clock, and the staff was sitting down to dinner.

Which was just as well, thought Sophy as she led Jane up the back stairs to the third floor. The Warings, with the privilege of old retainers, would certainly have asked a question or two if they had seen Jane so pale and distraught. And the last thing Sophy wanted was to answer questions. She had far too many herself and not a single answer.

"Sophy." Jane gasped for breath. "I know the ostler is lying. But it's so awful! I think I'm going to be sick."

"No, you're not. This is not the time to indulge in spasms or sickness. If this preposterous tale is true, Andrew will need our help."

Jane clung to the banister on the third floor landing. "But what can we do?"

"I'll think of something. First, however, we must change."

During the next few minutes, Sophy was kept busy looking after Jane, who had started to shake and shiver. She helped her into a dry gown and brushed the tangled mop of honey-brown hair— tasks that occupied her hands but kept her mind free to worry about Andrew.

But, perhaps, she need not worry at all. Lucian had gone to his brother's aid—where else would he have rushed in such a hurry? Lucian would tell the Admiralty men that they had made a stupid mistake. That the so-called witness made a mistake. Lucian would not let Andrew end up in Newgate or any other hell of a prison simply because a set of bubble-heads didn't know what they were doing.

But what if Lucian had not gone to the Admiralty? And what if Andrew was already in prison?

She did not want to share her troubled thoughts with Jane. The poor girl was distressed enough. But she had to ask one question.

"Did your father say where they took Andrew?"

"No." Jane's eyes widened in dawning horror. "Surely you don't think . . . *prison?* Sophy, I couldn't bear it! I—"

A deep blush spread over her pale face and receded just as quickly. Her chin went up. "I love him, Sophy."

"If you love him, you can bear anything. But I don't think we have to worry about prison. He'll be at the Admiralty," Sophy said staunchly. "You'll see."

Rain drummed against the windows, and it grew so dark that Sophy had to light the lamps before changing her own gown.

At last they were presentable once more, Jane in rose-colored muslin and Sophy in blue.

"Come along, Jane. What we need now is a cup of tea while we decide what to do. I suspect Lucian took the carriage. I could ask Miss Addie if she needs the barouche this afternoon, but I don't think we should tell her where we want to go."

"Tea sounds lovely." Jane followed Sophy downstairs. "If you don't mind my asking, where do we want to go?"

"Why, Jane!" Sophy cast an incredulous look over her shoulder. "To the Admiralty, of course. And I must say it is too bad of you not to have come in a carriage."

Jane was about to apologize, but the imperative rapping of the knocker made her gasp. "Andrew! Sophy, could it be—"

"Andrew doesn't knock. But, perhaps, a messenger."

They picked up their skirts and flew down the last dozen steps, coming to a breathless stop in the entrance hall just as Lieutenant Lord Christopher Hawthorne was admitted by the footman. Rivulets of water streamed from Kit's shako and pelisse.

"Janey!" He stared at his sister in astonishment. "Didn't know you were here."

"Of course you didn't. You weren't supposed to. I left the house without telling anyone."

Kit's eyes narrowed as he studied Jane's pale face. "You heard Father, didn't you? In which case, I suppose, I need not worry how to break the news to Lucian."

Sophy, aware of the footman who stood waiting to receive the visitor's dripping shako, said quickly, "It's all humbug! A misunderstanding, I'm sure. Lucian has already left—he didn't say where, but he must have gone to the Admiralty. Kit, would you please drive Jane and me to the Admiralty?"

"In this downpour? Sophy, take a peek out the door! You'll drown in the curricle."

"Fudge! It's nothing more than a drizzle."

Kit protested, pointed out that, if Lucian had gone, there was no need for anyone else to visit the Admiralty. But he was no match for Sophy at her most determined.

The footman was sent off for galoshes and weather-proof cloaks, and before long Jane and Sophy were seated in the curricle beside Kit, who told his tiger to run along and get dried off in Lord Northrop's kitchen.

"I don't know why I'm doing this," Kit grumbled as he flicked the reins. "It's madness. And, no doubt, Lucian will have my head for it."

"You're doing this because of Andrew." Sophy squeezed closer to Jane, who was riding bodkin. "How anyone at the Admiralty can be so stupid as to arrest him! It's—it's simply too idiotic for words."

"Listen, Sophy. I don't believe for a moment that Andrew killed Peter. But there's no getting around it that an ostler of Brompton's Livery Stables identified Andrew as the man who drew steel on Peter Marston. The Admiralty people were only doing their duty when they arrested him. As soon as they've found the right fellow, Andrew will be released."

"I don't intend to wait until they've found the right fellow. Drive to the livery stables, Kit! I'll speak to that ostler myself."

"And I will, too," said Jane.

Kit rolled his eyes. But he'd do anything rather than burst in at the Admiralty with two emotion-laden young ladies in tow. If he knew Sophy, she'd be voluble and direct to the point in letting everyone, including the First Lord himself, know they were blundering fools and had made a stupid mistake.

And Jane— He knew that stormy look of old. He wasn't even surprised to see it again after months of demureness. The question was what had so suddenly revived the passionate side of her nature. The injustice of Andrew's arrest . . . or Andrew himself?

He glanced at her, the determined set of mouth and chin, then returned his attention to the horses. There'd be time later for questions. For now, he'd just be grateful that the rain was letting up.

"'Twas Mr. Payne I saw."

Barker, head ostler at Brompton's Livery Stables,

faced them in Mr. Brompton's office to the right of the main gate in Jermyn Street.

"Many a time have I seen Mr. Payne when he stabled his horses here. I'd reckernize that yeller hair an' the blue driving coat with the gold buttons any day."

"It wasn't day, though," Sophy pointed out. "It was dark. You'd have to have cat's eyes to notice distinctive marks of identification."

"Don't know about 'stinctive marks of whatever you said, miss. But I saw those buttons, big as saucers and with that same squiggly pattern Mr. Payne has on his."

"Even if you saw gold or gilded buttons in the dark," said Jane, "I doubt you could distinguish the etching."

Barker cast a look at Lord Christopher—one man appealing to another for support against the unreasonable female of the species. "There's a lantern over the side gate where I saw the stabbing. Perhaps yer lordship would take a look?"

"We'll *all* take a look," said Sophy.

"We have ter cross the yard, miss. Puddles 'n' muck's deep after a rain."

Sophy was undeterred. "Never mind the puddles. We'll all go."

"Yes," Jane said firmly. Hitching her skirts as if she were already ankle deep in muck and mire, she marched from the office.

The rain had stopped, but the sky was still dark and gloomy. Which, thought Sophy, was somehow appropriate to the circumstances.

"'Twas quiet that night," said Barker as they approached the narrow, arched pedestrian gate set in a stretch of brick wall between one of the stables and a coach house. "Not much ter do. 'Twas my turn to blow a cloud, an' I go to step out this here side gate 'cause Mr. Brompton don't allow us to smoke our pipes inside the yard. Had one stable burn down six or seven years back an' lost twenty horses."

"Do you recall what time it was when you decided to smoke your pipe?" asked Sophy.

"Aye, that I do. St. James's struck ten when I left the stables. I stopped for a word with one o' the lads, but it couldn't have been more'n five after ten when I opens the gate."

They had reached the pedestrian gate. Barker lifted the latch and pulled. The gate creaked softly.

"See?" Stepping out into York Street, he pointed to a fair-sized lantern swinging from an iron hook above the arch. "It's lit ever' night at dusk, an' Wednesday night was no exception. An' what I saw fair made my blood run cold."

"What exactly did you see?" asked Sophy.

"I saw Mr. Payne stabbing a man."

"You're lying!" Pointing an accusing finger at the ostler, Jane said angrily, "If you had seen anything at all, you would have reported the murder on Wednesday night. But you never spoke up until the men from the Admiralty came looking for a witness. Do you think the Admiralty will pay a reward? Is that why you made up this preposterous tale?"

"Janey." Kit put an arm around his sister's shoulders. "Let Mr. Barker tell his story."

"Yes, indeed," said Sophy. "I want to know every detail. But I'm as curious as Jane about Mr. Barker's reason for keeping quiet until today."

"'Cause until today I didn't know the dead man was a government man. I thought he was a footpad, trying to hold up Mr. Payne. An' if Mr. Payne rid us o' one o' them thugs, so much the better."

Kit gave a snort. "The dead man was a gentleman. You could hardly have mistaken him for a footpad."

"Ho! I couldn't, could I? An' how d'you think the footpads operate in St. James's? I tell ye how, my lord. By dressing as gentlemen. That's how."

"Very well," said Sophy. "We'll let that pass for now. Just tell us—"

Barker, having the bit well between the teeth, interrupted unceremoniously. "O' course, if I could've seen the face o' the man that got stabbed, I would have known he weren't no footpad. But he had his back to me, an' he was crouched over as if ready ter spring at Mr. Payne. I never knew until this morning that he was Lieutenant Marston."

"So you knew Marston as well as Payne," said Kit. "I suppose Lieutenant Marston also stabled his horses here?"

"A nice little mare, that's all he has. Always hired one o' our hacks when he had ter go out o' town."

"Very likely," said Sophy. "But that is not important now. Mr. Barker, you said you did not recognize Lieutenant Marston that night because he had his back to you. But you clearly recognized the assailant?"

"I tell you I did. 'Twas Mr. Payne."

"You saw his face?"

"I saw him. He was standing right there." Barker pointed to a spot about six or eight feet south of the gate.

"Did he see you?"

"Not then, I don't think. He was twisting off that silver top o' his walking stick, an' out comes that long blade."

"Wait!" Sophy frowned. "I supposed Peter was

stabbed with a knife or a dagger. But a blade out of a walking stick? How odd."

"A sword stick," said Kit. "It's not uncommon. My father has one."

Barker nodded. "Aye, my lord. That's what it'd be. A sword stick. And afore I can draw breath, Mr. Payne stabs the lieutenant."

"It wasn't Mr. Payne!" Jane's eyes flashed. "You're lying!"

"Now, miss, you've got no call ter take that tone with me. I've told what I saw, an' I'll stick with it."

Sophy gave Jane's hand a warning squeeze. They must wear the ostler out with questions, not antagonize him with accusations.

"Mr. Barker, how can you be certain it was Mr. Payne? You saw his face?"

"It were Mr. Payne all right."

"Did he wear a hat?" asked Kit.

"Aye."

Sophy pounced. "Then how can you say you saw the man's blond hair? The spot where you said he stood could not have caught sufficient lantern light to show the hair color even if he had been bareheaded."

"I saw what I saw, an' it was Mr. Payne," Barker said stubbornly.

Sophy wanted to shake him.

Jane, with a visible effort to stay calm, said, "Mr. Barker, are you saying you opened the gate and simply stood there, watching a murder, and you never made an effort to stop the killer?"

"Miss, I was so flabbergasted I couldn't have moved or called out for anything. There I was, wanting to blow a cloud, an' I see what I think's a footpad getting his just desserts by Mr. Payne, as fine a young gent as I know. If I could've moved, I'd have shut the gate and loped off quicker 'n you can blink an eye."

"The gate creaks," said Sophy. "The men must have heard it. They would have been alerted. They would have turned to see—"

"Not necessarily." Kit gave the gate a push. "The creak is slight. I'd say nothing short of a pistol shot or a carriage going full tilt can distract two men intent on deathly combat."

"That's right, my lord. Don't know if Mr. Payne saw me earlier, but it wasn't until after he'd stabbed the lieutenant that he suddenly swung the sword at me. Gave me a fair turn, it did. I was rooted to the spot, but I yells, 'Mr. Payne! Gorblimey! I ain't no footpad. Don't ye reckernize me, Mr. Payne? It's me, Barker!'"

Sophy's heart thudded painfully. "Go on, Mr. Barker. Don't keep us on tenterhooks. He must have said or done something."

"Nothing, miss."

"Dammit, man!" Kit glared at the ostler. "Do you take us for fools?"

"He never said nothing," Barker insisted. "Just tucks his chin under, an' then his shoulders starts ter shake like he's chuckling to hisself. Pokes the sword back in the walking stick an' calm as a cucumber goes to the dead man an' tugs some papers out o' his pocket. Then off he goes."

Sophy's eyes met Kit's. Papers taken from Peter Marston's pocket could only have been the vital orders to Admiral Calder.

"Where did he go?" asked Jane.

Barker pointed south, in the direction of St.

James's Square. "Mr. Payne went that way, back to his chambers."

"Bloody hell," muttered Kit.

"Dash it! Don't swear." Sophy scowled at him. "I wouldn't mind so much if every now and then a lady were permitted to indulge in a bit of swearing herself. But since she's not—"

She turned to the ostler. "Mr. Barker, you may have witnessed the murder of Lieutenant Marston, but you did not see Mr. Payne do the deed."

Barker drew himself up. "Miss, I like Mr. Payne. When I thought he snuffed a footpad, I says to myself, it's none o' your business, Barker. But when a gent comes from the Admiralty this morning and says it's Lieutenant Marston that got snuffed, an' he was carrying some vital papers that have gone amissing, I had to speak up."

"I agree," said Sophy. "You had to tell them what you saw. But you never saw Mr. Payne. You merely think you did."

"'Twas Mr. Payne. I'd know him anywhere. Besides, miss, there was two other gents from the Admiralty that come in a while later with Mr. Payne hisself. An' Mr. Payne never denies nothing. Never says I'm wrong."

Fifteen

"Why?" asked Sophy. "Why on earth did Andrew not speak up?"

"We'll soon find out," Kit said grimly.

Once more, they crowded into the curricle. Silent and glum between her brother and Sophy, Jane weighed the chances of a strong, healthy man getting carried off suddenly by a fatal illness—or perhaps an injury? Surely, even an experienced head ostler could get kicked in the head by a maddened horse and die. And if Barker were no more, he could no longer insist he had seen Andrew.

Kit flicked the whip. The pair of matched bays obediently sprang forward, carrying them at a fair clip toward Whitehall.

Sophy looked up when they passed the two lodging houses where Andrew and Louis de Bouvier had chambers. Andrew on the second floor in the building on the right, Louis on the second floor to her left. The windows, blank and blind, stared mockingly back at her.

Two attacks in York Street . . . the one on Peter Marston ending in death. Horace had been lucky.

Two young gentlemen, living in York Street. One suspected of Peter's murder. Yet, the other was arrested.

"It's absurd!" said Sophy. "They could not, *would not,* arrest Andrew on the ostler's evidence. Why, it's not evidence at all! It's mere speculation."

"Just what I was thinking." Without a check, Kit guided the horses into St. James's Square. "The arrest makes no sense, especially since the Board of Admiralty had as good as decided that Louis de Bouvier killed Peter. My father said the only point on which they disagreed was whether Peter peddled information to Louis."

"I refuse to believe it of Peter. He wanted nothing more than to be aboard ship again and fight the French. He would not, because he found himself landlocked, turn about and aid and abet the enemy. And then there is Peter's servant. Also stabbed. And Horace was attacked today. I suppose those clever minds at the Admiralty suspect—"

"What does it all matter?" interrupted Jane, roused from her dark thoughts. "Peter Marston is dead. His servant is dead. Suspicion can no longer hurt them. But it can hurt Andrew. It has! It got him arrested!"

Kit gave his sister an indulgent look. "You didn't listen, Janey. What we've been saying is that he would not have been arrested on suspicion alone."

"The investigators must have found something else," said Sophy. "Some piece of evidence, which they think points to Andrew. It is nonsense, of course. Andrew is not a murderer."

"If only we could prove it," said Jane. "Perhaps we can look for a witness who saw Andrew somewhere far away from York Street?"

A gleam lit in Sophy's eye. "Payne House. Andrew was there when Horace came to report Peter's death. That was shortly after eleven." The gleam dimmed. "But who knows how long before that he was in the house."

"Dash it, Sophy!" Kit kept his attention fixed on the busy traffic of Charing Cross. "It doesn't help if no one knows when Andrew arrived at Payne House. Probably makes it look worse."

"The butler," said Jane. "Or the footman. They would know."

Sophy shook her head. "Lucian doesn't find it necessary to keep a footman stationed in the entrance hall after eight. Unless he's entertaining."

"Emancipation of the servant," Kit muttered. "Always told Lucian his revolutionary notions would lead to no good."

"Revolutionary!" Sophy bristled. She might tease Lucian about the reforms he introduced in the household, but she would brook no criticism from anyone. "And that from the man who sends his tiger to parish school twice a week."

"Thought that would get a rise out of you. And about time, too. Between you and Janey, you make me think I'm driving a hearse."

"Sorry, Kit. I'm a bit on edge."

Jane scowled at her brother. "You're not exactly brimming with cheer either."

"And that's why we'll have no more talk about what cannot help Andrew until we've learned what *can.*"

"In which case," said Sophy, "you had better drive a bit faster. You've always boasted that these bays of yours—"

She broke off, staring at a carriage that had turned from Whitehall into Charing Cross and now passed them in the opposite direction. A carriage with the coat of arms of the viscounts

Northrop emblazoned on the door and with two gentlemen inside.

"Turn back, Kit! There's Lucian and Andrew. Hurry up and turn around!"

"Dash it, Sophy! I cannot turn in the middle of Charing Cross."

"I can. Just hand me the ribbons!"

"You're mad." Kit tightened his grip on the reins and pulled back, slowing the horses for the turn into Whitehall.

"Turn around!" Sophy urged again.

He did not answer but, seeing an opening in the oncoming traffic, swung sharply right. It would have been an easy turn into Whitehall, but the full turn Sophy demanded was nigh impossible. If he were driving anything other his cherished bays harnessed to a curricle he would not have made the attempt.

Holding his breath, he completed the turn with barely an inch to spare between the near wheel and the corner street post and entered the stream of westbound Charing Cross traffic a nose length ahead of a dray pulled by six sturdy Clydesdales.

"Well done," Sophy said approvingly. "Thank you, Kit."

"Was it truly Andrew in the carriage?" asked Jane, unimpressed by her brother's prowess as a whip.

"Yes, it was," said Sophy. "And Lucian. And with Samuel Trueblood on the box, we shouldn't have any trouble catching up."

"No doubt you'd like me to spring 'em." Kit raised a quizzing brow. "Or else you'll demand the ribbons again?"

"Spring 'em, by all means. I have complete confidence in your ability to catch up."

"If it was Andrew," said Jane, bouncing on the seat, "it must mean that he's been released. Do hurry, Kit! Can you not go faster?"

Kit did his best to catch up with Lucian and Andrew, but one carriage stubbornly remained between the curricle and the Northrop coach.

"It doesn't matter," said Sophy when the three vehicles turned one after the other into Piccadilly. "It's not as if there's any danger of losing them."

"No," said Kit. "It's obvious that they're headed for Payne House. I just wonder who's trailing them. I don't like the looks of that carriage."

"Neither do I." In fact, the sight of the dust-gray vehicle filled Sophy with trepidation. "It looks—" Her nose wrinkled. "It looks like a dashed government coach."

"It looks ugly," said Jane. "But who gives a straw? Andrew is free, and that's all that matters."

But Andrew was not free.

"He is *what?*" demanded Sophy.

They stood in the center of the downstairs drawing room, Lord Barham, Lucian, Andrew, Kit, Jane, Sophy, and two men in unobtrusive gray and black, who had arrived with the First Lord of Admiralty in the dust-gray carriage.

Poker-faced, Lord Barham repeated, "Andrew is a prisoner of the crown, Miss Bancroft, placed in the custody of his brother."

"On my parole of honor not to attempt an escape," Andrew supplied.

He was pale. His hair stood on end as though he had repeatedly raked his fingers through it. But a smile, boyish, irrepressible, lurked in his eyes.

"This is nonsense!" Sophy said indignantly. "Ridiculous!"

"Utter rubbish!" said Jane.

She could say no more. Her brother placed a hand over her mouth, clasped her arm with the other, and drew her toward the fireplace.

"Hush, Janey! Or I'll take you outside," Kit warned.

Her gaze on Andrew, the girl subsided.

"It's a ruse!" Sophy looked at Lucian, standing beside his brother. "Isn't it?" she demanded. "A trick to catch the true culprit. The same trick you employed to catch Callums's murderer."

Lucian, too, was pale. His hair, as dark as Andrew's was fair, might not stand on edge, but neither was it immaculate. Unlike Andrew, Lucian did not have a smile lurking in his eyes.

"No ruse, Sophy." His voice was flat, lifeless, dousing the spark of hope in her breast.

"Andrew will have the run of house and garden," said Lord Barham. "If, however, he attempts to leave the premises, he will be apprehended and taken to Newgate."

"By those . . . gentlemen?" Sophy indicated the two men in plain gray coats and black knee breeches who had not moved a step beyond the closed drawing room door but stood, still and silent, like Horse Guards on duty at Whitehall.

She looked at Lucian again. She wanted to reach out to him, but something in his eyes, an expression at once forbidding and pained, stopped her.

For an instant, the span of a heartbeat, she had the eerie sensation that she did not know him at all, this man she was to marry in two months' time and who had told her mere hours ago that he loved her to distraction.

She blinked, and the feeling was gone.

She said, "Dash it, Lucian! This is outrageous. Lord Barham's threats, the gaolers he installed in *your* house! Surely, there is something you can do!"

"I'm afraid there's nothing Northrop can do," Lord Barham said soothingly.

That it was the First Lord who replied irritated her. She was scarcely aware of Jane and Kit standing still and silent near the fireplace. Only of Lord Barham, dominating the scene. Of Andrew, who carefully avoided her eye.

And of Lucian, pale and distant.

"Believe me, Miss Bancroft," said Barham. "I did not authorize Andrew's arrest on a whim."

Sophy tore her gaze away from Lucian. This farce had gone far enough, and what she had to do to stop it was better done if she could not see Lucian's face.

"Lord Barham, no matter what that ostler thinks he saw, Andrew did not murder Peter Marston. He could not have done so."

"I did not act on the ostler's testimony, although it supports what my men have uncovered. Miss Bancroft, we now have evidence, concrete evidence, implicating Andrew."

"That is impossible, sir. Andrew was here, at Payne House." She did not blink, nor did her face grow warm. "I spoke with him about ten o'clock while I was waiting for Miss Addie to get ready for the Dolwyn ball."

Someone gasped; probably Jane. Sophy did not bother to look. She listened for an explosion from Lucian. It did not come. Fingers crossed and hidden in the folds of her gown, she kept her eyes on the First Lord of Admiralty.

"Ah, yes," said Lord Barham. "The Dolwyn ball. I was there myself. A sumptuous affair. Unfortunately, I didn't get to enjoy it. Was closeted in the library most of the time."

He smiled at Sophy. "My dear young lady, I'd like nothing better than to accept your word that Andrew was here at the time Peter Marston was killed. But I cannot."

Her bosom swelled. "Why not?"

"About an hour ago, I sent a man to interview the staff here. No one saw Andrew that night until eleven-thirty or a little later, when the butler making his rounds encountered both Andrew and Horace as they left Andrew's study."

"It's not unusual that the staff was unaware of his presence. Andrew has his own key. And, during one of my first nights here, I saw Horace letting himself into the house."

"I know all about Andrew's habit of letting himself in and disappearing in his study or in his chambers with none the wiser. I even know about Horace's key. No, Miss Bancroft, that is not what makes me question your word."

He paused. "It's Horace, whom my man found recuperating upstairs. Horace swears that Andrew was in the York Street chambers, sleeping off the effects of a bottle of brandy, until roused with the news of Peter's death."

Sophy closed her eyes. A pox on Horace and his ill-advised meddling!

"Yes, Miss Bancroft. It doesn't even make sense, does it? But that's loyalty. I believe you possess not a small amount yourself."

"Sir!" She might seethe with chagrin but voice and posture indicated only outraged dignity. "No one has ever questioned my word."

Andrew cut in. "Say no more, Sophy. I already confessed there's no one to support my claim that I came here after leaving the Admiralty. That was about eight-thirty." A corner of his mouth curled in a wry grin. "Giving me plenty of time to stab Peter."

"For goodness' sake, Andrew!" She rounded on him. "Don't even say it in jest! And why the dickens didn't you speak up sooner? I hate getting caught in a fib."

She faced Lord Barham again. "But that is neither here nor there. It is utterly ridiculous to arrest Andrew. I suppose, you'll be charging him next with the attack on Horace!"

Two quick strides brought Lucian to her. He clasped her hands.

"Before you say anything else, my love, let me tell you why Lord Barham had no option but to have Andrew arrested."

"Go ahead." She set her jaw firmly. "The sooner I know, the sooner I can go about disproving whatever evidence he thinks he has."

"Sophy, the dispatches for Admiral Calder, which Peter was to have carried to Bournemouth, were found in the safe in Andrew's study in York Street."

Sixteen

Sophy stared at Lucian. He would not jest about such a serious matter—and yet, how could it be true?

"Poppycock!" said Kit

"It's a lie!" cried Jane. She ran to Andrew's side. "Say it's a lie! Say it, Andrew!"

"I'm afraid it's true all right. Sorry, Jane."

As he might have done to his three-year-old niece, Andrew tweaked one of Jane's curls. Her face flamed, but Andrew did not notice. He was looking at Lord Barham.

"Somehow or other, I've landed myself quite thoroughly in the basket. Haven't I, sir?"

Sophy felt Lucian's grip tighten on her hands. It was true, then. The papers . . . the vital orders for Admiral Calder to stop Villeneuve from joining the invasion force at Boulogne . . . in Andrew's safe.

Her mind refused to consider the implications. There was an explanation. There must be. In a moment, when her thoughts stopped spinning, she'd think of it.

She became aware of Lord Barham's voice. He was talking to her. Hadn't he said more than enough already?

But he was only taking his leave. Pressing duties at the Admiralty.

"Good-bye, Miss Bancroft." With old-fashioned courtesy, he bowed over her hand. "I shall see you tomorrow, and, I'm glad to say, under happier circumstances."

"Will Andrew be cleared tomorrow, Lord Barham? It is the only happy circumstance I can envision."

"I was thinking of the Piercepoint picnic, Miss Bancroft."

"That," she said coldly, "is a pleasure I shall forgo if Andrew cannot be there."

Lucian slipped an arm around her waist. "Nonsense," he said, fueling the indignation she tried hard to keep in check. "Of course we shall attend the picnic."

"I hope it rains," said Jane.

A sentiment with which Sophy was in wholehearted agreement.

Lord Barham bowed once more and moved off.

Andrew followed him. "I shall see you out, sir."

The two silent men in gray and black fell into step behind Andrew. A moment later, Jane rushed off, muttering something unintelligible.

Kit gave Lucian an apologetic look. "Don't think I'm running out on you, old boy. But right now I had better see what Jane is up to."

The door had not quite closed behind him when Sophy gave indignation full rein.

"Just what the dickens is the matter with everyone?" She whirled out of the shelter of Lucian's arm and faced him. "Lord Barham and the rest of them at the Admiralty! How can they believe that

Andrew killed Peter? Or that he took those stupid dispatches?"

"The papers were in Andrew's safe," Lucian said reasonably.

"There is an explanation." Sophy dismissed the papers with a wave of her hand. "But Andrew! How can he take his arrest so lightly? How can he smile and say he had plenty of time to stab Peter? And then he sees Lord Barham out. As if the man were a cherished visitor!"

"Sophy, love. Don't get all in a stew about this. You'll see—"

"I *am* in a stew. And so should you be. Your brother arrested for murder—" She broke off, white-faced. "My God, Lucian! It's worse than a murder charge. It's *treason.*"

"Yes."

"You're taking it calmly." Her gaze fixed on him with painful intensity. "Lucian! Surely you don't believe that Andrew— No, of course you don't!"

She passed a hand across her throbbing forehead. "Forgive me. If I weren't in such a dither, I would never have asked such a stupid question."

"You didn't ask it. Not quite." His mouth twitched in the attempt of a smile, but a troubled frown darkened his eyes. "Sophy, I'm calm because I realize that matters could be much worse."

"*Worse?* How—"

"Andrew could be in prison."

"Releasing him on his parole was the least Lord Barham could do! And, I'm sure, you had to pledge your word as well."

Lucian drew her onto a sofa and once more possessed himself of her hands. "I'm afraid Andrew's word alone, or mine, would not have been sufficient surety for the Board of Admiralty. It was Sir Jermyn's pledge that made the difference."

"Sir Jermyn on our side! I'm glad." She tugged to free her hands, but he would not let go.

"Lucian, we must get to work. We must find out how those dratted papers got into Andrew's safe. We must question the clerks at the Admiralty. The clerks who heard Sir Jermyn refer to the letters from Rye!"

"Sophy—"

"And, since we have nothing at present to link Louis de Bouvier to Peter's death," she continued ruthlessly, "it is time to turn our attention to the stabbing of Peter's unfortunate servant. Somebody in St. Martin's Lane must have seen or heard something."

"We interrogated everyone on the premises and in the neighboring houses. No one was seen during the time in question, save for a mysterious lady. Cloaked and veiled. You may draw your own conclusion."

Unblushing, she did. "Somebody's mistress, who doesn't want to be recognized."

"Married, no doubt."

"Did one of the lodgers acknowledge a visit from the mysterious lady?"

"No, and that's why the search for her continues. The dagger is not exclusively a man's weapon."

His words made her shiver. Or did she feel cold because, for some obscure reason, at the very same moment she thought of Véronique de Bouvier?

"Lucian, couldn't the weapon have been a sword stick?"

"Not according to the Admiralty experts. And

their opinion is supported by the coroner. Apparently, not all stab wounds look the same."

"Still . . ." She hesitated. "What if the veiled lady was a man in disguise?"

"The possibility has not been ruled out."

"It won't hurt to question the lodgers in Peter's building again."

She rose when he did not reply, pulling him with her.

"We must start somewhere. How else will we find the killer? And the traitor, if he's not the same person. How long do we have before the trial?"

"No date has been set." Again, a deep, troubled frown darkened Lucian's eyes. "Sophy, we cannot go to St. Martin's Lane. Lord Barham has forbidden any interference with the investigation."

"Interference! How dare he!"

"He is in charge."

After a pregnant pause, she said, "Lord Barham is not in charge of me or my actions. I made him no promises."

"Barham is aware of your interest in solving crimes. His men have instructions to intervene if you insist—"

She interrupted, her color high. "They would stop me? Intolerable! But I shall find a way. If need be, I'll get a writ from Sir Jermyn, giving me leave to investigate."

"Sir Jermyn does not have the power to override the First Lord's orders. Besides, he is on his way to Wales. A sudden family emergency requires his immediate attention."

"Dash it, Lucian! It sounds like a conspiracy."

He shook his head. "You're suspicious of everything and everyone."

"A helpful trait in an investigation."

"Not in this one. For goodness' sake, stay out of it!"

Her breath caught. "Are you forbidding me to try to find the true culprit?"

"Would you obey if I did?"

"No."

The calm facade crumbled. His mouth tightened, giving his face a stern, harsh look. Once more, he was a stranger, a man whose thoughts and feelings were alien.

"Devil a bit, Sophy! I'm asking you to leave well enough alone."

"Well enough?"

Again, she tried to tug her hands free. Lucian tightened his grip as if to demonstrate that he could stop her by physical strength if need be.

"What is well enough in this situation?" she demanded. "Peter's death? Andrew's arrest? Or that Louis de Bouvier is free and clear of suspicion?"

"Stop pulling away and listen to me!" Exasperation sharpened his voice. "Despite Andrew's arrest, the Admiralty men are still working on the case."

"Their work leaves much to be desired if all they can come up with is evidence *against* Andrew."

"Give them time. The majority of the Board may be convinced of Andrew's guilt, but the investigators are not. They had to report their findings, but they know Andrew, and they're not at all happy."

She gave him an incredulous look. "So you want me to do nothing?"

"Yes."

"I cannot believe it! Lucian, you're gambling with your brother's life."

He flinched. Finally letting go of her hands, he half turned away from her.

"Credit me with more sense than that," he said brusquely. "I know what I'm doing, Sophy. And I know what I'm asking of you."

"Do you? What am I supposed to do? Smile and attend picnics?"

"It would help." Quite calm again, he faced her. "And you might spend time with Jonathan."

"*Jonathan?*" She had to think who Jonathan was. "What does *he* have to do with Andrew?"

"Nothing, of course. But, let me remind you, he has very much to do with our marriage plans. Where is Jonathan, by the way?"

"On his way back to Rose Manor, I hope."

"If you'll remember, I invited him to stay a few days." Lucian's tone softened. "I thought you might show him around, introduce him to some of our friends."

"You want me to dance attendance on Jonathan? *Now?*" Arms akimbo, she scowled at him. "Lucian, you did that on purpose! You invited him to get me out of the way."

He did not deny it. Smoothly, persuasively, as if he wouldn't dream of making an unreasonable demand, he said, "Surely it isn't asking too much to take Jonathan about. Once he realizes that no scandal is attached to our betrothal—"

"Lud! When he hears about Andrew, he'll send a notice to the *Gazette* immediately, declaring our engagement null and void."

"He does not have to know. At least not until the investigation is closed."

"Jonathan is not deaf! If he stays in town, he'll visit the clubs and hear—"

"Sophy, listen. Lord Barham may have ordered Andrew's arrest, but he *is* a gentleman. Until Andrew is arraigned for trial, he is, at Barham's suggestion, 'confined to his rooms with a sudden attack of influenza.' That's what Aunt Addie and the household will be told, and it's what we shall put about among the members of the *ton.*"

"It won't fudge. All of the Admiralty staff know the truth. There will be gossip, rumors."

"The Paynes have weathered rumor and gossip before. Just make certain Jonathan knows there's no gossip about *us.*"

It was on the tip of her tongue to tell Lucian he could dashed well take Jonathan about town himself, when she remembered her invitation to Linnet and Caroline and Jonathan's wife. Jonathan was already in a rage over her refusal to return to Rose Manor. If she antagonized him further, he would definitely not let Caro visit her.

"Very well, I'll bear-lead Jonathan. But not until *after* I've spoken with Andrew about the papers in the safe."

"Sounds reasonable." Lucian looked relieved. "Any other conditions?"

"I'll have a word with Horace." Her brow darkened. "To have put me on the spot with as stupid a lie as I've heard!"

"Apropos Horace—" Lucian went to open the door. "He's been placed under arrest as well and mustn't leave this house."

Sophy sniffed. "No doubt, they think he's Andrew's accomplice."

"At present, he's charged with perjury."

Her step faltered, but she caught herself immediately. She was a Bancroft of Rose Manor, unafraid of the shadow of prison looming ahead.

Keeping her tone light, she said, "Perhaps Lord Barham would like to arrest me, too?"

A rare boyish smile, much like Andrew's, flashed across Lucian's face. "He'd have me to reckon with. Pistols at dawn, Sophy. Barham wouldn't dare."

Responding to his lightened mood, she curtsied. "I'm honored, my lord."

She stepped into the entrance hall. Her gaze immediately fell on the taller and thinner of the men in gray and black. The sight of sinewy legs in clocked stockings recalled to mind the Bow Street Runner hired by Lucian after the murder of Miss Addie's abigail. Tarp had not been very convincing in the disguise of a footman.

"I suppose," she said wryly, "compliments of the Admiralty, we have acquired a third footman?"

The gleam in Lucian's eye told her that he, too, remembered.

The man in the plain gray coat bowed. "Sedgewicke, at your service, miss. I'm the hall porter."

Sophy murmured, for Lucian's ears alone, "My! Aren't we getting fancy in the revolutionary Whig viscount's household?"

Then, to Sedgewicke, she said, "And your colleague? What position does he hold?"

Sedgewicke's face lost none of its impassivity, but, she thought, she saw the glimmer of a twinkle in his disconcertingly sharp eyes.

"Adam is a designer, miss. He's seeing to the refurbishing of the gazebo."

"Adam . . ." She glanced around the marble splendor of the entrance hall, designed by the illustrious Robert Adam. "How appropriate."

"Yes, miss. That's what we figured."

She could not help but like Sedgewicke, despite her poor opinion of Admiralty men.

"Where did Mr. Payne go?" asked Lucian.

"To his study, my lord. Lieutenant Hawthorne and the young lady accompanied him."

"In that case, let's first see Horace," said Sophy, walking toward the stairs.

She had not set foot on it when she heard a door open at the back of the entrance hall, then Jonathan's voice.

"No, Miss Addie. Don't trouble yourself. I'll find Sophia if I have to turn the house upside-down. The chit has no manners! I've always said so. And why Northrop wants her is more than I can tell."

Starting up the stairs, Sophy shot a look over her shoulder. "Do something, Lucian! I won't be bothered with him now, so don't you try to fob him off on me."

"I shan't." To her indignation, Lucian chuckled. "But I'd like to demonstrate to him why I want you."

She increased her pace. "Hush! He'll hear you."

"Sophia! Northrop!" Jonathan thundered from the back of the entrance hall.

Taking two steps at a time, Sophy reached the top of the first flight of stairs and hurried up the second to the yellow chamber, where Horace was installed.

For the present, Lucian must deal with Jonathan. She had more important matters to tend.

Seventeen

Sophy knew, of course, that she could not escape Jonathan forever, but after reading Horace a homily on the foolishness of lies in general and *his* lie to the Admiralty investigators in particular, she felt buoyed enough to face anything. Even Jonathan's company at dinner. Even, if Lucian insisted, the Piercepoint picnic in Richmond Park the following day, Saturday. And Jonathan's presence there.

Only the prospect of Sunday loomed dauntingly. Sunday was a day devoted by even the more frivolous members of the *ton* to church and quiet family gatherings. At home. There would be no escape from her cousin.

But, at least, she would have Lucian's support.

Descending from the second floor, she stopped at the foot of the stairs when she saw Lucian coming up from the entrance hall. He looked pensive and grave, but his expression brightened as soon as he caught sight of her.

He bounded up the last few steps, caught her in his arms, and lifted her off her feet.

"Sophy, my love. I hope you've not totally devastated Horace."

"If anyone deserved a tongue lashing, it was Horace for telling such a disastrous fib."

"Of course *you* would never tell a fib?"

She looked into his eyes and felt her heart tumble in her breast. How she enjoyed his nearness, the hard pressure of his arms.

"That was different."

"Oh?"

"*My* fib could have worked if he had not told his."

Chuckling softly, he set her down. "Don't be too hard on him. We need Horace since Andrew is destined to suffer from influenza."

"Yes, I see your point. I don't imagine Andrew will be an easy patient."

"And don't forget, Horace is also confined to the house. Nursing Andrew is as good an explanation as any for his presence here."

"You've thought of everything—except how to get Andrew cleared."

The grave look she had observed when he mounted the stairs returned. "I've just seen Kit and Jane out. If you want to speak to Andrew, this would be a good opportunity."

"Will you come, too?"

"Are you inviting me?"

"Most cordially."

As they walked down the corridor to Andrew's study, Sophy asked, "What have you done with Jonathan? Fobbed him off on poor Miss Addie again?"

"Nothing as horrid as that. Your cousin was put out that he had no carriage other than the traveling chaise at his disposal, and he wanted to spend an hour or two at White's. So I made him a loan of my phaeton."

"Lud! He'll overturn it. There's no one as cow-handed as Jonathan."

"*Cow-handed*? Where the deuce did you pick up that expression?"

"Papa used it all the time. Particularly to describe Jonathan's handling of the ribbons."

"No doubt your father was correct. But Jonathan won't overturn the phaeton. Not with one of my grooms at his side."

Lucian opened the door to Andrew's study, and Jonathan was instantly forgotten at the sight of Andrew, immersed in work at his desk and giving no more than a nod and a distracted smile to his worried future sister-in-law.

Seated stiff and poker-straight in front of the desk, Sophy pounded Andrew with questions and listened in growing exasperation to his absent-minded replies as he kept scribbling on diverse sheets of paper scattered all over the desk top. Finally, she snatched the pencil from his fingers.

"Andrew, you are the most unsatisfactory witness in his own defense I have ever encountered. Now, will you *please* pay attention!"

"Yes, ma'am." Andrew lounged back in the deep leather chair. "Wouldn't want to get my knuckles rapped."

"You deserve a whipping," she said crossly. "Do be serious."

Lucian, perched on the corner of the desk, said, "My love, why won't you believe me when I say that the situation is not as bad as it seems? We are in excellent trim as long as the investigation continues."

She thought of Sedgewicke, posing as hall porter. She liked his eyes, sharp and keen. If he were investigating . . . but he had been set to guard the prisoner, to make sure he didn't escape. As if Andrew's parole wasn't good enough!

"Rubbish!" she said. "We cannot depend on anyone's efforts but our own."

Pushing back the chair and crossing his long legs, Andrew looked at Lucian. "Can't wait for Helen to get back from China. I wonder if she knew what she was doing when she sent Sophy to you to play governess to her offspring. She always used to say—"

"Never mind what Helen used to say," Lucian interrupted. "You had better do as Sophy says and give her your attention. Immediately."

Curiosity made Sophy magnanimous. "I've waited this long, I can wait a moment longer. Andrew, what did Lady Simpson say?"

Andrew avoided his brother's eye. "Helen used to tease Lucian about his preference for quiet, unassuming young ladies. She said he never paid attention to a pert miss because he couldn't bear to have a female stand up to him."

"Andrew!"

The tone of Lucian's voice was ominous, but his graceless brother was unimpressed.

"And if fate ever forced him to deal with a young lady as stubborn as he is himself, Helen said, he wouldn't know how to handle her."

Intrigued, Sophy asked, "And you suspect Lady Simpson played fate?"

"No doubt about it."

"May I remind you two," said Lucian, "that we have *serious* business to discuss?"

Sophy gave him a sidelong look. "You did not think so a moment ago. What made you change your mind?"

"The frivolous nature of the present discussion. Helen is a feather-head. And what she said about me and stubborn young ladies proves the point. Now, let's get back to the safe in York Street."

"Yes, indeed," said Andrew, glancing at the clock on the mantel. "If you've more questions, Sophy, fire away. I don't have all night. Not if I want to get these dratted letters decoded."

Sophy was instantly diverted from Lady Simpson's predictions. There was only one set of letters everyone had been talking about all day.

"The letters taken off the drowned man in Rye?" she asked, incredulous. "Lord Barham has you working on the code—after arresting you for treason?"

Lucian stirred restlessly and looked as if he were about to speak.

Andrew forestalled him. "Lud, yes! Who else could do it? And with two men to guard me, I'll hardly pass the information to whoever was meant to receive it. Will I, now?"

"Don't be flippant." But she could only shake her head at the vagaries of the gentlemen in charge at Whitehall.

"Dash it, Sophy!" muttered Andrew. "What will you have me do? Beat my breast and tear out my hair?"

Before she could reply, Lucian prompted, "Sophy, you wanted to know if Peter was aware of the safe in Andrew's study."

"Was he?" Eagerly she leaned across the desk. "Peter was in your study and wrote you a note. Telling you nothing you did not already know. I think it entirely possible that the seemingly meaningless note was a clue. Peter wanted to alert you, and then—"

"Didn't alert me to anything," said Andrew. "Made me think he must've been a bit on the go."

"Fudge! Peter wouldn't drink when he knew he'd be riding to Bournemouth at dawn. No, he wanted to give you a clue, and then he put the papers in the safe. *If* he knew about the safe."

"He may have known about it. The bloody thing is right there behind the mirror over the mantel. I may have put papers away during one of Peter's visits, or I may even have shown him the blasted thing. How am I supposed to remember?"

"Andrew, it's important."

"No, it ain't, Sophy. Even if he knew it was there, he couldn't use it. Only Horace and I have keys."

"He could have picked the lock. I understand, if you know how, it isn't all that difficult."

"You try it. That safe was made by Richard Scott. He swears it's not only fireproof, but the special lever lock is unpickable."

"Besides," said Lucian, "the ostler saw the assailant pluck the papers from Peter's pocket. Which means Peter still had them *after* he left Andrew's chambers."

This seemed unanswerable.

Sophy, however, wasn't at a loss for long. "It simply means that the papers taken by the assailant were not the orders for Admiral Calder. Those papers could have been anything . . . even the dispatches from Lord Nelson. They're still missing, aren't they?"

Silence fell over the study.

Finally, Sophy said, "Let's forget about the papers in Peter's pocket. They're not important at the moment. We know it wasn't Andrew who took them."

"But it is highly improbable," said Lucian, "that

the assailant entered Andrew's apartment after slaying Peter and put them in the safe."

Andrew nodded. "He would have had to wait until Horace left. And then, how would he have opened the safe without a key?"

"You truly believe the lock unpickable?" asked Lucian. "I was inclined to side with Sophy, that Peter himself must have placed the orders in the safe."

"I tell you, it's impossible without a key. I know. I once tried to pick the lock when I mislaid the key."

"There's another possibility," said Sophy. "Peter left the papers on the desk, and Horace put them in the safe."

"Horace?" A gleam of amusement lit in Lucian's eye. "I wondered when you would suggest him as a suspect. He was your first choice when—"

"I did not say he was a suspect." Her look reproached. "And you know very well I suspected him as the jewel thief only very briefly and not at all after Callums was murdered."

"He'd make a great suspect, though," said Andrew. "Just think! Horace saw Peter last. And he found the body."

"But he was attacked for the Rye letters," said Lucian. "Now, if the letters were actually stolen from him, I'd have suggested that he staged the attack to make himself look innocent. Alas—"

"Stop it!" Sophy cut in. "I know neither one of you takes me seriously, but this is not a time for bantering."

"Don't scowl." Lucian brushed a finger across her forehead. "It isn't all banter. In a case of treason, anyone even remotely connected with the Admiralty must be considered under suspicion."

Sophy nodded. She had pointed out very much the same to Horace when she named Sir Jermyn and Lord Dolwyn as possible suspects who might have betrayed the existence of the Rye letters.

"Very well. But all I'm saying for now is, Horace has a key to the safe. He may have taken the papers off the desk and put them away."

"He does clean up after me." Andrew smiled disarmingly. "I have the habit of stuffing papers under the blotter. Offends old Horace's sense of orderliness."

"I'll speak to him. And if he did not—" Sophy took a deep breath. "Don't worry, Andrew. Somehow or other, I'll find out how those dratted orders got into your safe."

She rose, refusing to be daunted by the sheer impossibility of the task she had set herself.

"And when I do," she said grimly, "Lord Barham will have to admit how wrong he was."

Neither Lucian nor Andrew offered an argument, and Sophy marched off, determined to prove her mettle.

She turned in the doorway. "One more question, Andrew. Why did you not speak up when the ostler identified you as the killer? Surely you could have convinced him that it wasn't you he saw."

A tinge of red crept into Andrew's face. "It was the driving coat Barker described. Or, rather, the buttons."

Lucian said, "When Andrew had the coat made, his tailor assured him the buttons were unique."

"But I don't have the coat now." Andrew's expression was part defiant, part sheepish. "I took Mademoiselle de Bouvier to Hampton Court on

Monday. On the way back we were caught in a storm. I gave her my coat."

"So Andrew said nothing rather than implicate the lady." Lucian gave Sophy a quizzical look. "I'd call it misplaced chivalry."

"Véronique had nothing to do with Peter's death. She loved him. But Louis——" Excitement took her breath away.

"Yes, it fits, doesn't it?" said Lucian. "Louis somehow got his hands on the coat, and he was wearing it when he killed Peter."

"Andrew!" Her voice rose. "Surely you're not keeping this from the Admiralty investigators? You must have told them. Or Lord Barham."

"Told the whole bloody Board when I saw they were going to order my arrest."

"And yet they arrested you?"

"I'm afraid they thought I was lying to save my skin."

"Fools!"

"Not fools," said Lucian. "Merely cautious, responsible men."

"Dash it, Lucian!" She glared at him. "How can you be so . . . *reasonable!*"

Sophy shut the study door with a snap. The matter was as simple as adding two and two. Louis took Andrew's coat and wore it when he killed Peter. No wonder he chuckled when Barker addressed him as Mr. Payne. Louis knew the masquerade had worked.

Only fools like the gentlemen at the Admiralty would refuse to see what had happened. And Lucian called them cautious. Responsible. Bah! There was a diplomat for you!

Her assistance in the investigation had been discouraged from the beginning. First by Lucian, who always worried too much about her. Then, without explanation or apology, by the First Lord of Admiralty. In fact, Lord Barham had not discouraged but outright forbidden her to participate in the investigation. And that after his agents arrested the wrong man!

Clearly, this was a time to defy even the head of the Admiralty. Since no one else made it a priority, it was up to her to prove either Louis's culpability or Andrew's innocence. And, until she had a notion how to go about the first, she'd concentrate on the latter by solving the puzzle of the papers in the York Street safe.

Horace, still out of charity with Sophy for the homily on lying to the Admiralty men, was no help at all. Indignantly, he said that, if he had seen the First Lord's orders for Admiral Calder lying around on anyone's desk, he wouldn't have put them in a safe but would have taken them straight to Mr. Andrew or to Sir Jermyn Leister.

Pressed, he admitted he had placed a stack of papers in the safe before leaving that night.

"But," he said, giving her a pugnacious look, "there weren't no orders for Admiral Calder."

And with that, Sophy had to be content.

She spent an hour with Miss Addie, who was happily engaged adding to the five names supplied by Sophy a long list of Payne relations and connections, friends and acquaintances, who must receive invitations to the wedding.

"But there are so many!" exclaimed Sophy, thumbing through several sheets of paper. "Lucian and I want a small wedding."

"It will be quite small and intimate," Miss Addie assured her. "I've trimmed the list down to a hundred and forty-four names."

Sophy had a mental image of a vast church, the pews on the groom's side filled to overcrowding. The bride's side gaping empty, save for the front pew occupied by Susannah and Jonathan, and by Miss Thiele, the governess who had prepared her for her present position. Linnet and Caroline might sit there, but, naturally, she wanted her sisters for bridesmaids.

Quickly, Sophy banished the image and, while Miss Addie explained the intricacies of the Payne family tree, put her mind to the problem of a lock mechanism that was supposedly unpickable.

It was an exercise in futility. Years ago, she had picked the lock of an old trunk in the attic of Rose Manor and the lock of the root cellar when Jonathan imprisoned Linnet and hid the key. But those were locks that even six-year-old George, Lucian's younger nephew, could have picked. A safe, apparently, was quite different. She did not even know what a lever lock was, let alone a special one. And that was what Andrew said secured the safe.

She was still grappling with the problem as she dressed for dinner and, subsequently, was the last to enter the dining room.

Andrew, since it had already been made known that he suffered from influenza, was not at the table. But Jonathan had returned from White's and sat on Miss Addie's left. Sophy, taking her seat on Lucian's right, only two empty chairs removed from Jonathan, could not help but overhear his complaints about the club's members, the wines served, the boorishness of the staff, and concluded that he had not been lucky at the gambling tables. He'd be in an impossible mood for days.

Impulsively, she placed a hand on Lucian's arm. "I know I said I'd spend time with Jonathan. But promise me that, at least tomorrow at the picnic and on Sunday, you won't desert me. Promise, Lucian!"

A warm light entered his eyes. "I have every intention of spending tomorrow and Sunday with you, my love. And Jonathan may go to the devil."

Alas for lovers' promises. Sophy had barely smiled her gratitude when the butler approached and presented a note on a silver tray.

"From the Foreign Office, my lord."

Eighteen

Lucian broke the seal.

"What does it say?" Sophy asked with foreboding.

"Oh, dear," said Miss Addie. "Not another emergency, Lucian?"

Jonathan, sampling the hock served with the fish course, said nothing.

Lucian refolded the note. He folded his napkin, set it beside the plate, and pushed back his chair. Rising, he drew Sophy's hand to his lips for a brief caress.

"I am sorry, my love. Mulgrave and Castlereagh require my assistance in a matter of extreme delicacy."

"Then, of course, you must go."

He looked as if he were about to say more but, in the end, bent and kissed her cheek. He bowed to his aunt and to Jonathan, muttered an excuse, and strode off. No one heard Sophy's sigh above the click of the closing door.

Matters of delicacy, Sophy knew from experience, tended to be drawn-out affairs and could keep Lucian occupied for several days. She was, therefore, not surprised if bitterly disappointed when the party setting out for the Piercepoint picnic the following day did not include her betrothed. She and Miss Addie went. Skeet. And, of course, Jonathan.

Fortunately, Miss Addie's presence had a softening effect on Sophy's cousin. He lost his temper only once, when Sophy introduced him to their hostess, and Skeet inadvertently stepped into what appeared to be the only puddle in all of Richmond Park remaining from the previous day's rain. A splash of muddy water landed on Jonathan's Hessian boots and triggered a diatribe that made those close enough to hear stare in astonishment. He gave not a thought to the boy's wet feet.

All in all, the picnic went better than Sophy had anticipated. No rumors about Andrew had spread, and her explanation for his absence—a sudden illness—was accepted without the raised brows she had feared.

Neither did Lucian's absence cause comment, save from the Misses Gabner, known for their mean dispositions and sharp tongues. These two young ladies, having completed their fourth unsuccessful season, slyly commiserated with Sophy for being so often deserted by her betrothed.

She would normally have ignored such catty remarks. But this time, perhaps because she was on edge on account of Andrew's precarious position or, perhaps, because she had begun to resent Lucian's frequent absences, she answered in kind.

"But, my dears!" Wide-eyed, and looking as if butter wouldn't melt in her mouth, she said, "Isn't it ever so much better to be occasionally deserted than to have no betrothed at all?"

Immediately ashamed of herself, she turned away to seek out Jane and bumped into Kit instead. His eyes danced with laughter. He had obviously overheard her.

"You'll make an excellent diplomatic wife," he said, chuckling.

"Perhaps I should apologize."

She looked back at the sisters, who turned up their noses and pointedly showed her their backs.

"Perhaps I won't, after all."

"Much better not. They'd only dig their claws in deeper. I suppose Mulgrave sent for Lucian to help calm down the Portuguese ambassador?"

"He is with Lord Mulgrave and Lord Castlereagh, but I know only that it's a matter of extreme delicacy. Do you know what the trouble is?"

"Nothing that hasn't happened before, only this time it looks a bit more serious." A gleam of excitement lit Kit's eyes. He offered his arm. "Let's walk and I'll tell you."

"Kit, is it—are we ready to send an expeditionary force?"

"That's what I'm hoping. The French are again pressing the regent of Portugal to declare war on us. So far Dom John has refused, but he's extremely worried. There are factions within Portugal—"

Kit broke off to bow to the Dowager Duchess of Wigmore, regally enthroned on a chair near the trestle tables laden with food and drink. Not content with a mere bow, the old lady beckoned imperiously.

"What's this I hear, Christopher?" she demanded. "You're finally off to war?"

"I wish it were so, ma'am. But for now, I can

only hope. Nothing has been decided. Lord Castlereagh—"

"Ah, bah!" her grace interrupted. "You'll not be leaving yet. Robert is a charming fellow—all Irishmen are. But why Pitt must appoint him Secretary for War, I'll never understand."

She peered shortsightedly at Sophy. "And you, miss? Have you a more definite date for the wedding than the last time we talked?"

"Yes, your grace. September the second."

"Good. Very good. Lucian is a nice boy. He'll make an excellent husband. When will I get the invitation?"

Sophy could not remember if the duchess's name was on Miss Addie's list, but anyone calling Lucian a nice boy must certainly be added.

"Miss Addie and I will be writing them in a week or two. I'll bring yours personally."

"You do that. Russell Square." The wrinkled face softened. "I like weddings. Hold on to him, gal. Lucian will go far. He'll be an ambassador before long. Mark my words."

Words, Sophy noted, that had certainly caught Jonathan's attention. Across a table spread with baked meats and crusty bread, he briefly met her quizzing gaze before he returned his attention to the food in front of him.

With the abruptness of the very old, the Dowager Duchess of Wigmore lost interest in Sophy and Kit and commanded the two footmen standing behind the chair to carry her into the shade.

The rest of the afternoon passed quickly and pleasantly. Kit, upon meeting Jonathan, volunteered to introduce him to his own and Lucian's friends, leaving Sophy free to join several young ladies in a rambling walk and a game of battledore and shuttlecock.

It might have been a lovely day, thought Sophy as she returned with Miss Addie and Skeet to the carriage, save for four circumstances.

Lucian had not been able to join the picnic party.

Andrew had to stay home, pretending to be ill.

Jane had hardly spoken to her, except to ask in an urgent undertone whether she might call on Sunday.

And neither Véronique nor Louis de Bouvier was present. The picnic would have been the perfect cover to put a vital question or two to the cousins without running the risk of getting stopped by Lord Barham's men.

But she received a consolation for the missed opportunity. Jonathan decided to join Kit and his friends for an evening at White's.

Lucian was still absent on Sunday, and Andrew was growing restless.

"Barham promised me the run of the house," Andrew complained to Sophy after a scold from Miss Addie, who had caught him sneaking off to his study and promptly sent him back to bed. It had taken two more attempts before he finally reached the study unobserved by aunt or staff.

"It's all of a piece!" said Sophy, her eye kindling. She was seated in front of the desk, Andrew behind it. "I've never seen such incompetence. First they arrest you. Then they want you to go on slaving for them as if nothing happened. And why must you be ill at all?"

Andrew's face turned red. "The scandal," he

muttered. "Think what it'd do to Lucian's career if it were known that his brother was arrested for treason. As a favor, Barham agreed to let me be ill until, uh, until—"

"Until they hang you?" she said cuttingly. "Or will you be shot?"

"Dammit, Sophy!" He jumped up and started to pace the narrow room. "Don't say things like that. It's enough to give a man the jitters."

"I'm sorry."

She joined him in front of the window. Laying a comforting hand on his sleeve, she said, "I'll have you cleared long before they set a trial date."

"I don't doubt you will." His cheerfulness could never be long depressed. A teasing gleam lit his eyes. "But can you save me from days, perhaps weeks of influenza?"

"I'll try."

Her mouth tightened as she remembered Lord Barham's self-assurance when he explained the reason for Andrew's arrest, his suaveness when he refused to accept her fib, which, after all, would have saved him from having to admit later that he made a mistake. It would give her no little satisfaction to inform Lord Barham that his "favor" was not the generous gesture he had intended.

As she turned to the door, her gaze fell on the desktop littered with paper. "I daresay it's too soon to ask if you've found anything in the Rye letters?"

"There seem to be several codes. I've broken one, and I believe I've caught on to another."

"Well? What did you learn?"

Andrew raked a hand through his hair. "Four

of the six letters are addressed to a Madame Victoire, each in care of a different hostelry. I found the first coded message in one of those letters. Nothing specific. Just the command to expedite operations."

"Four letters addressed to this Madame Victoire. It would seem she's someone important."

"My guess is she's the head of French agents in town," said Andrew, his voice strangely choked.

"Madame Victoire . . ." Sophy's voice trailed as the same thought that must have struck Andrew occurred to her. But it couldn't be. Could it?

She met his troubled look. "Oh, no, Andrew! I cannot believe it's a code name for Véronique. If she's involved at all, she's no more than a go-between. I wouldn't worry if I were you."

He colored painfully, but said with an attempt at flippancy, "What'll you wager? The hostelries are watched. So we may have an answer soon."

"A code name does not necessarily reflect the agent's sex. And wouldn't it be rather unusual to have a female in charge?"

"A bit unusual, perhaps. But not unheard of."

"If you must have a wager, I'll give you odds that Louis is Madame Victoire."

Sophy left, more perturbed than she wanted Andrew to know. To give her thoughts a less troublesome direction, she went to her chamber for the pleasure of penning a note to the First Lord of Admiralty.

She did not mince words but stated baldly that Lord Barham could not expect the household to accept "influenza" while Andrew was wearing himself out decoding the letters from Rye.

Furthermore, she wrote, it upset Miss Addie to

see her nephew running about the house while suffering from influenza. And Andrew, naturally, insisted on freedom of house and garden, as promised by Lord Barham. Perhaps the First Lord would be kind enough to think of a different illness? If he could not, Sophy would be happy to resolve the matter for him.

The footman sent off with the note returned promptly with a reply.

Lord Barham apologized for his shortsightedness. He should have realized that influenza wouldn't do. If it was convenient, Sir Alastair Block, Barham's own physician, would call later that day and make a fresh diagnosis of Andrew's illness.

As to the letters from Rye, Lord Barham thanked Miss Bancroft for bringing the matter to his attention. The letters should not have been left in Andrew's possessions and he would personally collect them Monday morning.

Frowning, Sophy read the missive a second time. Something bothered her. The First Lord's reply was as polite as she could wish. And yet—

She crumpled the note. If the situation weren't so serious, she'd think Lord Barham was playing a game with her. She truly must do something about her imagination.

Jane came to Payne House late Sunday afternoon. Flushed and disheveled, she stormed into the sitting room where Miss Addie, with Skeet's assistance, was unraveling a shawl she had knitted far too loose and too long, and Sophy was doing her best to entertain Jonathan with a rubber of piquet.

But since Sophy was winning, Jonathan was not in a happy frame of mind.

Breathless, Jane curtsied to Miss Addie on the sofa by the window, then turned to the card players seated at a low table in front of the empty hearth.

"Sophy! Please, may I have a word with you? In private."

Jonathan, who had ponderously risen to his feet, said irritably, "Sophia is busy. You cannot speak with her until we've finished the rubber."

Ignoring him, Sophy addressed Miss Addie. "If you've no objections, ma'am, Skeet can take my place with Jonathan."

"No objections at all." Miss Addie took the ball of wool Skeet had wound. She smiled at the boy. "You like piquet, don't you, dear? But mind you don't play higher than penny points."

"No, Miss Addie."

Skeet shot a calculating look at Jonathan. "How about it, guv'nor? When I've finished Miss Sophy's game, will you play me? A penny a point and sixpence for the rubber."

While Jonathan hesitated, torn between pride, forbidding him to play against a mere child, and greed, telling him to teach the impertinent urchin a much needed lesson, Sophy and Jane slipped from the room.

"What is the matter?" Sophy ushered the visitor into the morning room and closed the door. "You look as if you ran all the way here."

"I did." Jane sank into a chair near the open French doors. She picked up one of the fashion plates depicting bridal gowns and fanned herself. "I ran because I've just had the most horrid row with Papa!"

"Gracious."

Sophy pulled up another chair. She had enjoyed many a good row with her papa, especially when she had saved and scrimped for some much needed improvement at Rose Manor and he demanded the money so he could back a horse that was bound to come in last. But she didn't think that was the kind of row Jane had with Lord Dolwyn.

"Your papa does not want you to visit Payne House. Is that it, Jane?"

"He is . . . outrageous and unreasonable! Can you believe it, Sophy? Papa is one of the men who accuse Andrew of killing Peter Marston and taking those dratted orders for Admiral Calder. Taking them to pass on to the French!"

"I believe it," Sophy said dryly.

Jane looked baffled and indignant. "Papa is convinced that Andrew is a *traitor!*"

"Yes, that seems to be the consensus at the Admiralty. Don't let it upset you, Jane. I'll prove them wrong."

"It's all very well for you to say so." Like Sophy, Jane did not believe in mincing words. "But I don't see how you can. That ostler swears he saw Andrew kill Peter. And the orders were in Andrew's safe."

"I know it looks bad—"

"I don't give a straw!"

Taking a deep breath, Jane fought for calm. "Even if Andrew swore on the Bible that he killed Peter Marston, I would not believe it. And I won't listen to Papa. I'll come to Payne House every day, whether he gives his permission or not. Sophy, I want to see Andrew. Will you help me?"

Sophy knew her duty. She knew what she should reply.

But these were extraordinary circumstances. No matter what new illness Lord Barham's physician devised, Andrew would be housebound and restless until she cleared his name. Jane, however, would not allow him to feel bored.

And neither would it hurt if a lively young lady took his mind off Véronique.

She rose. "Come along, Jane. Andrew is in his study."

Nineteen

Sophy did not want to feel guilty about Jane. She told her conscience there was no reason to make a fuss. She had instructed Horace not to leave the study under any circumstances as long as Jane was there with Andrew. On top of that, she had told Horace to order the carriage when the young lady was ready to leave.

The last order put her in a quandary when shortly after six-thirty a note arrived from Véronique de Bouvier, requesting Sophy's presence at the Serpentine in Hyde Park. Immediately.

Véronique . . . Madame Victoire?

Despite her reassuring words to Andrew, Sophy believed it possible. And nothing would keep her from the rendezvous.

It would be daylight for a while yet, but on a Sunday, Hyde Park was overrun with apprentices and clerks and their lady friends. It was not a place Sophy would have chosen for a meeting unless she had a trusted coachman and a groom with her.

But she had designated the carriage for Jane's use, and she would not go back on her word. She'd drive herself in Lucian's phaeton or, if Samuel Trueblood had the impertinence to refuse harnessing the phaeton for her, she'd take a hackney. Skeet could go with her.

Skeet, flushed from a win of eighteen shillings and ninepence, agreed readily to accompany Sophy. Not so Samuel Trueblood, who personally brought the phaeton to the front door. Samuel tried to talk her out of driving anywhere on a Sunday evening. Then, when Sophy lost her temper and told him to get down, that she'd drive herself, he relented but ordered the ferociously scowling little page to stay home.

"I'll have me hands full lookin' after you, Miss Sophy, without having ter chase after this will-o'-the-wisp."

Sophy hesitated. She had wanted Skeet to walk with her and Véronique. But of how much help could a boy be if an amorous clerk or journeyman decided that two unaccompanied young ladies were fair game? And during her talk with Véronique, Skeet would be very much in the way.

"Skeet, I have a different assignment for you. Something more important than walking with me and Mademoiselle de Bouvier."

The scowl did not ease. He shot her a suspicious look. "For instance?"

"I need someone clever, who can keep my cousin from worrying Miss Addie when he finds out that I've left the house."

Skeet, always protective of his adored Miss Addie, drew himself up. "Nobody worries Miss Addie when I'm around. What else d'you need me to do, Miss Sophy?"

Sophy thought of Jane in Andrew's study, with only Horace as a chaperon. She did not regret what she had done, but her conscience refused to be quiet.

"Lady Jane went upstairs to keep Mr. Andrew company. She feels sorry for him—"

"Aye." Skeet's grin spread from one saucer-like ear to the other. "Poor Mr. Andrew. A sicker man I never saw in all my life."

Samuel Trueblood grumbled. "Miss Sophy, how much longer are ye planning ter keep the horses standing?"

Taking her seat beside the coachman, Sophy gave Skeet a stern look. "Mr. Andrew is ill. How ill, we'll know when the physician has seen him later today. Meanwhile, do you think you can get Miss Addie to keep Lady Jane company and not send Mr. Andrew to bed?"

"A tall order, Miss Sophy." Skeet's voice faded as the phaeton started to roll. "But I'll do my best."

Samuel drove at a pace he considered befitting a young lady of quality, leaving Sophy at leisure to remember Lucian's warning not to interfere in the investigation. If she ignored the warning, the Admiralty men had orders to stop her.

She turned around several times to check if the phaeton was followed, but no carriage stayed persistently behind them.

A church clock struck the half hour past seven when Samuel Trueblood guided the phaeton through Chesterfield Gate.

"I hope mamzelle is right where we can see her from the carriageway," he said. "I'm not of a mind to let ye go traipsin' all over, looking for her."

But Véronique was in plain sight, feeding the

ducks on the Serpentine where the carriageway followed the water's edge for several hundred yards.

That did not seem to suit Samuel either. He stopped with obvious reluctance.

"Mind, ye don't linger, Miss Sophy. It'll be dusk afore long."

"Not for an hour. Now, drive on," said Sophy, getting down from the high perch.

She glanced at the crowd of Sunday revelers. A few couples with small children, but mostly young girls, maids, seamstresses, shop assistants. Some with their beaux, some alone or in groups of three and four. And a multitude of young men spruced up in their Sunday best and looking for a conquest.

Perhaps, among the swaggering young men lurked an Admiralty investigator, keeping an eye on Mademoiselle de Bouvier, cousin of the man who had been, before Andrew's arrest, the prime suspect for the murder of Peter Marston.

Be that as it may. Sophy's chin assumed a determined tilt. No one would stop her from speaking to Véronique.

Samuel Trueblood was still waiting.

"Drive on, Samuel. And if it gives you peace of mind, you may pass by every five minutes or so. Mademoiselle de Bouvier and I will not venture far."

"An' so I should hope, miss. This ain't no place for well-bred young ladies."

"It's Hyde Park, Samuel. Not Seven Dials. We'll come to no harm."

Sophy turned and went to meet Véronique, who had left the ducks and was coming toward her. Sophy's breath caught. Véronique had been pale and on edge when last she saw her in Russell Street, but the woman approaching her looked drawn and haggard. Lifeless—except for the dark eyes, burning with a feverish glitter.

Madame Victoire? Surely not. The head of French agents would be ice cold, deadly calm. Perturbed, Sophy covered the last few steps at a run.

"Are you ill?"

"No."

Véronique touched Sophy's arm, steering her away from children fighting noisily over a ball. A short distance away, four giggling young ladies vacated a bench, which Sophy and Véronique promptly took over.

They faced the water, stained red and orange by the setting sun. Several yards behind them ran the carriageway, not too close that they would be hit by bits of flying gravel from a passing vehicle, but close enough to hail Samuel Trueblood with no more than a raised hand.

About twenty paces to their left, a half dozen young men lounged on the grass. Their laughter drew Sophy's attention, but after watching them awhile, she decided they were what they appeared to be and not Admiralty investigators in disguise. She looked at Véronique, who was strangely silent for a woman who sent an urgent summons.

"Why did you want to see me?"

"I need to know— Sophy, you must tell me what you know of Peter's death. The truth, if you please! Not the tale about the footpad."

The sun touched one side of Véronique's face and hair as she turned pleading eyes on Sophy. It was thick, long hair, elaborately curled and styled. But the rich, fiery highlights that should have ignited in the mahogany curls were missing.

A wig.

Sophy barely stopped herself from speaking the thought aloud. Another simple solution. The ostler had been correct after all. Only, the blond locks he saw on the assailant and identified as Andrew's were nothing but a wig set atop Louis's dark hair. But how to prove it?

"Sophy! Why are you staring at me? Is it so impossible what I ask? Or are you, as you once told me when I caught you staring, preoccupied?"

"I was momentarily diverted. But never mind that now. Véronique, the last time we met you weren't sure any longer that we could be friends. Why, then, did you send for me?"

"Because I trust you. And," Véronique added hesitantly, almost reluctantly, "I like you."

As during their first meeting, Sophy warmed toward the French girl.

"I like you, too. But I don't know if I can trust you. There have been so many inconsistencies, half truths, in what you told me that I don't quite know what to believe."

"Ask me about what you do not understand," Véronique said urgently. "I shall try to tell you the truth. I must make you trust me! There is no one else I can ask to tell me about Peter."

"Very well, I shall ask you. Does Louis have a blond wig?"

"A wig?" Véronique frowned in confusion. *"A perruque?"*

"Blond."

"I do not understand why you ask, but I do not think Louis has a wig. A wig is no longer fashionable with young gentlemen, and Louis would not wish to appear behind the times."

"No doubt you're right." Absently, Sophy noted that the noisy children had taken their ball and joined their parents in packing the leftovers of a picnic into a basket. "Let me ask another question."

"Am I being catechized?" Véronique attempted a smile, but it came across as a tight little grimace on her taut features. "As you were by the Dowager Duchess of Wigmore at the Dolwyn ball?"

"I'll probably not ask half as many questions. Véronique, did Andrew give you his driving coat? Royal blue with—"

"With many capes and the biggest gilded buttons I have ever seen. But, yes. He let me wear it when it rained on our return from Hampton Court." Véronique's eyes narrowed. "Sophy, are you worried that Mr. Payne is paying too much attention to me? I assure you, he only imagines himself in love with me. He will get over it very soon."

"I agree. At three-and-twenty, a young gentleman let loose among the ladies is like a child in a toymaker's shop," said wise, twenty-year-old Sophy. "I don't worry about that. I only wanted to know if you still have that coat."

"But, no! When the coat was dry I gave it to Louis to return to Mr. Payne. That was the very next day, the day before the Dolwyn ball. Are you saying—"

"That Andrew does not have it. Yes, Véronique, that's what I'm saying. Do you know where Louis was before he went to the Dolwyn ball and what time he left town that night?"

It seemed impossible that Véronique could turn any paler, but she did, her skin looking like parchment.

"How you do jump about," she murmured. "Let me think. Before the Dolwyn ball . . . I do not know where Louis was. He did not say and I did not ask. But I know he planned to leave town that night, as soon as he had changed clothes. Sophy, will you tell me why you are asking these questions?"

Sophy's hands clenched the wooden seat of the bench. Pray God, she was doing the right thing!

"Friday morning, Andrew was arrested for the murder of Peter Marston. He was arrested because a witness saw a blond man wearing Andrew's coat pull a blade from his walking stick and stab Peter."

In the silence following her words, Sophy heard the crunch of gravel as a carriage passed behind them. But she did not turn to see if it was Samuel Trueblood with the phaeton.

"Mon dieu," whispered Véronique. "It is true, then. It is just as I feared."

"What is true?"

"Louis. He killed Peter." Véronique's face contorted in pain. "But why? *Why?*"

Twenty

Sophy's heart raced. She had expected much from this meeting, but not an outright admission that Véronique, too, suspected Louis. It wouldn't do, however, to betray astonishment or surprise.

"I hoped *you* could tell me why Peter was killed."

"I do not know. Or, perhaps—" Eyes fixed on the darkening water of the Serpentine, Véronique shook her head. "Give me a moment to collect myself. I must think."

Again, Sophy heard the crunch of hooves and wheels on the carriageway behind them. This time, she turned. But it wasn't the phaeton with Samuel Trueblood on the high-perched seat. It was an open barouche, the coachman on the box, and a female on the forward seat.

Sophy stared at the woman. Gray cloak, wide-brimmed gray silk hat, a thick veil like a silver-gray cloud falling from the hat's brim to her shoulders. Something tugged at Sophy's memory, yet she did not recall having encountered the woman before. She was still searching her mind when the barouche swung off the main carriageway and disappeared from view.

She turned back to Véronique, lost in thought and gazing at the shadowed water.

"Véronique?"

The French girl gave a start.

"Will you at least tell me what brought you to the conclusion that it was your cousin who stabbed Peter?"

"I apologize. I should never have asked you to meet me."

"If you had not, I would have called on you tomorrow and asked about the cloak."

Jerkily, Véronique got to her feet. "I should never even have gone to you the morning I worried about Peter. Sophy, you must promise to stay away from me."

"Why? What will happen if I don't?"

"Nothing! Nothing will happen," Véronique said just a bit too vehemently to be convincing. "But I should not have involved you in my affairs."

"Are you Madame Victoire?"

She recoiled. "*Grâce!* How do you know about Madáme Victoire?"

"Never mind how." Sophy tugged at Véronique's arm. "Sit down and tell me if you are this Madame Victoire, who, I take it, is the head of French agents."

"No, of course I am not Madame Victoire." As if her legs would no longer support her, Véronique sank onto the bench.

"Louis?"

"No."

Sophy gave her a sharp look, which Véronique met squarely.

"No, Sophy, I am not trying to protect Louis. I assure you he is almost as afraid of Madame Victoire as I am."

A wave of disappointment washed over Sophy.

She did not question Véronique's statement, but neither did she allow it to daunt her.

"Who, then, is this mysterious person?"

"No one knows." The evening was warm, but Véronique shivered. "Sophy, I cannot like this. You should not have heard of Madame Victoire. It is dangerous knowledge."

"Only ignorance can hurt." Slowly, Sophy released her grip on Véronique's wrist. "Especially ignorance about someone I like."

Véronique said nothing, but a tinge of red crept into her pale face.

"Even if you're not Madame Victoire, you're a spy. Aren't you, Véronique?"

"Yes."

"And you wanted to become better acquainted with me because you hoped I'd tell you what Lucian and Andrew learn at Whitehall."

"Yes."

Sophy nodded. It was not strange that the truth hurt—even though she had suspected it. But the vast emptiness inside was worse than pain. Whatever the outcome of this affair, she and Véronique could not be friends.

Her gaze strayed to the group of young men who, moments ago, had lounged on the grass. They had risen and now sauntered off, still laughing and jesting, in the direction of Chesterfield Gate. Everyone else, the families and young girls, had left. Sophy and Véronique were alone. And dusk was falling.

A large scrap of paper drifted leisurely over the ground and came to rest at Sophy's feet. It was smudged and wrinkled, but she caught the words

Emperor Napoleon . . . Liberty, Equality . . . Loyal Supporters across the Channel.

One of the pamphlets Napoleon Bonaparte had sent to England the previous year and again this past spring. He promised positions of rank to those Englishmen who would fight for his cause when he crossed the Channel with his invasion force.

What humbug! He might have saved himself the trouble it must have cost to smuggle the pamphlets into England. No one in his right mind would fight for the French emperor.

Sophy was about to suggest that they stroll along the carriageway until Samuel Trueblood drove up, when Véronique started to speak.

"I was seventeen, about to be presented, when Maman and I fell victim to the scarlet fever. We were very ill, and Maman never quite recovered. What little money Papa had left was needed for the physician and for the cures in Bath and Tunbridge Wells prescribed for Maman."

She gave Sophy a rueful look. "I do not know if you can understand what it is like to be a penniless girl in London during the Season?"

"I understand. After the betrothal, when Lucian wished to introduce me to society, I had my 'governess' gowns and not a penny to spare for more elegant dresses, let alone a ball gown."

"But Viscount Northrop, he is rich. He has bought you gowns, has he not? For I see you always dressed very beautifully."

"In England, a lady can accept gowns only from her husband."

"So it is in France. If you will pardon my curiosity, how, then, did you contrive?"

"I was quite set on braving society in drab grays

and browns, but Lucian outdid himself in diplomacy." A hint of mischief lurked in Sophy's eyes. "He persuaded my guardian—and don't ask me how—to assume payment of the school fees for my sisters. Then he paid me the full year's salary so I could shop for dress materials."

"Materials? You sew your own gowns?"

"I do. But Miss Addie is the artist who designs and cuts them."

Véronique sighed. "It is what I should have done. But I was young and foolish. I wanted pin money enough to keep me in gowns from Madame Bertin." She touched one of her long curls. In a low voice, she added, "And in *perruques*. The illness, you see, it took my hair."

Her throat tight with compassion, Sophy nodded.

"I wanted to cut a dash and capture the heart of a wealthy nobleman," said Véronique. "After watching me mope at home that first Season, the following spring Louis suggested ways I could earn the pin money I craved."

"Through spying."

"It did not seem like spying then. I was invited to a great many of the *ton* parties, and I heard so many things. I never asked questions, but Englishmen are very fond of discussing affairs of state, especially when they can boast of their knowledge to a young lady. I had only to listen and repeat the gossip to Louis."

Sophy thought of Sir Jermyn, who never guarded his tongue.

"But then you met Peter Marston. And you persuaded him to give you copies of secret documents?"

"No! I admit, I tried to get specific information from Mr. Payne and from you. Because Madame

Victoire was pressing me. But I never asked Peter for documents. And when I carried messages, they were always from Louis to Peter. Never the other way around. But Louis told me that Peter was . . . helping us."

"I don't believe it. Peter lost a foot in service to his king and country. He would not aid Napoleon Bonaparte and his agents."

Sophy rose. She had wanted answers to her questions; she mustn't complain if they did not fit the picture she had of the young naval lieutenant.

She peered into the gathering dusk, but there was no sign of Samuel Trueblood and the phaeton. How strange, when he had fussed and fretted about her visit to the park.

Véronique said, "But it is indisputable that Peter obeyed the orders of Madame Victoire."

"Why is it indisputable?"

"It was Madame Victoire who demanded that he propose marriage to me."

Sophy tore her gaze from the carriageway. "It was not a love match?"

"On my part, yes. But Peter agreed only with the greatest reluctance. I hoped," Véronique added softly, "he would feel differently after we were married."

How sad. But Sophy did not say so aloud.

The drumbeat of hooves and the rattle of wheels disrupted the stillness of the evening. Two horses, judged Sophy. Driven at a gallop. It could not be Samuel.

But it was Samuel Trueblood after all, who pulled up with the phaeton.

"Miss Sophy! Are ye ready ter leave?"

A lady did not shout. However, these were extra-ordinary circumstances.

"Yes, Samuel! We'll be there in a moment."

Sophy turned to Véronique, who had risen and stood waiting to take her leave.

"Véronique, will you come with me to St. Martin's Lane?"

"Peter's chambers? Why? The gentlemen from the Admiralty removed all his papers on the morning they discovered the body of Peter's servant. You will not find anything that would help prove or disprove his connection with Madame Victoire."

"Yes, I suspected as much."

Sophy hesitated. She was taking a gamble, counting on Véronique's willingness to help convict Peter's killer.

"The gentlemen from the Admiralty are so absolutely convinced of Andrew's guilt, they would refuse to believe that the witness to the stabbing saw Andrew's driving coat, but not Andrew himself. However, if I find the proof that Louis killed Peter's man, then even the bubble-heads at Whitehall must acknowledge a connection."

"What you're asking is— Sophy, I do not know if I can help you. Already, I doubt my own mind. I do not want to believe that Louis killed Peter."

Abruptly, Véronique turned her back on Sophy.

"And yet—I remember, when I told him that Peter was dead, all he asked was, what is known about the murderer and what is known about the way Peter was killed."

"He wanted to be certain his masquerade had worked. He knew there was a witness, and it must have disconcerted him that a footpad was blamed."

"And the message he wanted me to give Peter! Louis is not clever, but he is wily."

"Louis gave you the message so that you would never suspect he had anything to do with Peter's death."

"So it seems."

Véronique's back stiffened. "Sophy, do you remember the morning you paid me a visit? Louis interrupted us. He was disconcerted by your presence—I could tell by his manner. He would never, otherwise, have admitted that he knew of Peter's plans to travel to Bournemouth. But Louis has a tendency to speak and act without considering the consequences."

"Véronique, how can you say you doubt your mind? You do believe it was Louis who killed Peter."

Once more, Véronique faced Sophy.

"What do you expect to find in St. Martin's Lane when all the Admiralty men discovered nothing?"

"But they did! Only, I fear, they don't have my imagination and pass it off as nothing."

"I do not understand."

"A suspicious stranger—a woman—was seen in Peter's lodging house that night. Don't you see, Véronique? If Louis disguised himself as Andrew to kill Peter, he would not hesitate to dress as a woman to kill Peter's man. And if I can prove it—"

"A woman was seen?"

In the deepening dusk Sophy could not read Véronique's expression, but she heard the sharp edge in her voice.

"Yes. And don't say my imagination is running away with me. It's what I tell myself, but on the other hand—"

"Miss Sophy!" shouted Samuel Trueblood. "It'll be pitch dark in a minute!"

Forgetting that Samuel might not be able to see, she waved to him.

To Véronique, she said hurriedly, "The Admiralty investigators believe she is a married woman who visited her lover in secret. She was heavily veiled. But I think it was—"

The Lady in Gray. The woman driving past in the open barouche, a cloud of silver-gray tulle veiling her face. But it was absurd to connect the two incidents. Veils were all the rage.

"I think it was Louis in the lodging house," Sophy said firmly. "He did not find the papers he wanted on Peter, so he came to look for them in his chambers."

"You are wrong." Véronique's voice was expressionless. "If there was a veiled woman in the lodging house the night the servant was killed, then it was Madame Victoire."

Sophy's mind reeled. *Absurd?*

"Madame Victoire. . ." Véronique shivered as if struck by a sudden chill and clasped her arms over her breasts. "Always cloaked and veiled. Always soft-spoken so that the listener cannot place the voice."

"Miss Sophy!" called Samuel.

Sophy wanted time to think, but there was none. Not now.

"Véronique, would Louis be in his chambers at this time?"

"I do not know."

Samuel Trueblood cracked his whip. To Sophy's amazement and consternation, the phaeton started toward her across the turf.

"Ain't waitin' a moment longer, Miss Sophy!

Been in service to the Paynes since I was a lad, an' I don't reckon ter lose me post if I can help it."

Véronique straightened.

"If Louis killed Peter, I will not let Mr. Payne be accused," she said, her voice strong, coldly determined. "And if you want to search Louis's chambers for the wig and driving coat, I shall help you."

Twenty-one

Sophy foresaw all sorts of difficulties that would bar the way to York Street, but, in the end, only the tight squeeze on a seat designed for two proved a slight but not insurmountable problem.

Samuel Trueblood, Sophy's most immediate concern, could have been obstreperous and refused to drive two young ladies into St. James's. But Samuel was in high dudgeon over an incident in Hyde Park that had forced him to leave Miss Sophy on her own far longer than his conscience permitted. A barouche, cutting into Samuel's path at a reckless speed, had locked wheels with the phaeton, and not until they turned into York Street did Samuel cease his diatribe against the hapless coachman in the park.

By then, Sophy had pointed out the building opposite Andrew's chambers where she wanted Samuel to stop, and it was too late for him to do anything but admonish her not to keep the horses standing more than a few minutes.

The next obstacle Sophy had feared was interference from Lord Barham's men as she approached the heavy, carved front door of Louis de Bouvier's lodging house. But no one, save for two swaggering blades who whistled as they passed

Sophy and Véronique, paid attention to the young ladies entering the building.

Sophy was elated. So much for Lord Barham's threat to stop her if she persisted in her investigation!

She thought of Lucian and the frown that would darken his eyes when he learned of her visit to Louis de Bouvier. Surely, he would understand?

As silent as they had been during the drive, Sophy and Véronique mounted the well-lit stairs to the second floor. But there, no one answered Véronique's knock.

They stared at each other.

"It is fortunate, of course, that Louis is not at home," Véronique said hesitantly.

"I suppose so." Sophy scowled at the door. It seemed her luck had run out. She was faced with an obstacle after all. "But I wish his valet were here to let us in."

"I do not understand what happened. Maurice does not like London. He never goes out. Unless," Véronique added pensively, "Louis sent him to make arrangements for a meeting with Madame Victoire."

But even Madame Victoire could not distract Sophy at this time. She directed a speculative look at the locked door.

"Is there a hall porter downstairs? He might have a key."

"I shall find out."

"Wait! There may be a better way."

"Sophy, what do you mean? What better way?"

"Hairpins. I don't need them for my short hair, but you must use hairpins."

"But yes!" For the first time that evening,

Véronique's face showed animation. She extracted a sturdy pin from her elaborate coiffure. "Do you know how to pick a lock, Sophy?"

"I've done it twice."

A lock on a trunk, and a lock securing a root cellar. Again Sophy looked at the door, this time rather doubtfully. Surely, a sturdy door lock could not be more difficult?

And what if Louis or his valet returned? Or one of the third floor residents went up or down the stairs?

Pshaw! She'd pit her wits against the treacherous Louis any time. And if they were caught by one of the lodgers, she'd think of some excuse.

Sophy inserted the pin. She wiggled and turned and twisted, and when Véronique pushed down the handle and opened the door, no one could have been more surprised than Sophy.

Again, they looked at each other.

"Go on," said Véronique.

Sophy's heart pounded. She had never hunted, but she had ridden in the steeplechase. And now she felt just as she did when she approached the last hurdle. Win or lose, she must take the jump.

She entered, followed closely by Véronique, who lit the lamp on the hall table, then shut the door.

The apartment was much like Andrew's across the street, where Lucian had taken Sophy once. A narrow hallway, serving as foyer, and two doors opening from the hallway on either side. The oak floor was worn but polished to a high sheen, and the table and mirror in the hall were dust free.

"The bedroom first, I think," said Véronique, pushing open the far door on the left.

As they thoroughly and efficiently searched

dresser, wardrobe, and chest of drawers, Sophy could not help but admire the single-mindedness with which Véronique went to work. She made a good partner in an investigation. Perhaps, when this affair was over . . .

"What about the vicomte, Véronique? The gentleman to whom your parents consider you betrothed. Would he still marry you if you are involved in a scandal?"

Véronique carefully closed a dresser drawer. "Would he marry me? Or are you asking will I marry him, now that Peter is dead?"

"I'm asking both, I suppose."

"But, perhaps, I will be shot or put in Newgate Prison."

Sophy's breath caught. "Surely not! Unless you lied to me about the extent of your involvement in the spying operation?"

"I did not lie."

"Well, then? Will you become the Vicomtesse Marchand?"

"Marchand will marry me even if there is a scandal. He lost his wife and three children to the guillotine and wants to start another family before it is too late."

"And you?"

"I, too, want children. Soon." A shadow crossed Véronique's face. "I am a practical Frenchwoman, Sophy. So, of course, I will marry him. He is not rich, but he can provide for a family—and for Maman and Papa when it becomes necessary."

"Being practical is rather like being responsible," said Sophy. "And responsibility is a word I've known and respected since childhood."

"Then you understand."

"Indeed. You must consider your parents. I have younger sisters to think of."

Sophy shut the wardrobe door. Perhaps she and Véronique could be friends after all. She would certainly do her best to persuade the First Lord of Admiralty not to have her arrested. Véronique had already paid dearly for her foolishness.

"Nothing here," she said.

Véronique's mouth tightened with determination. "The spare room next."

Sophy picked up the lamp and followed Véronique to the chamber across the hall.

And there, in the wardrobe, hung Andrew's royal blue driving coat with the large gilded buttons. A blond wig rested in an old hat box, thrust into the farthest corner of the wardrobe.

"*Mon dieu!* For my parents' sake I had still hoped I was wrong."

"And I for your sake," said Sophy.

"I shall never forgive him. Never!" Véronique stared at the driving coat. "He kept it, the fool. How sure he is of himself."

Pale and shaken, Véronique followed Sophy out of the building into the street, inadequately lit by a flambeau above the door.

"I do not think it was wise to leave the coat and wig upstairs," Véronique said, not for the first time.

"But I tell you, Lord Barham would not believe that Louis had the articles in his possession, unless he saw them with his own eyes in Louis's apartment."

"Surely, your word—"

"Lord Barham," Sophy said stiffly, "does not accept the word of a lady."

Samuel Trueblood had turned the phaeton and was waiting in front of the building even though it placed him in the path of oncoming vehicles. He climbed down to allow Sophy and Véronique to take their seats without having to step into the street.

"Do you plan to take me to Lord Barham?" asked Véronique, gathering her skirts to make room for Sophy on the high perch.

"If you don't mind, I'd like you to come to Payne House, so we can tell Andrew."

"Hurry, Miss Sophy," said Samuel. "Hear that carriage? I'd like to be out o' the way afore we gets run over."

Indeed, Sophy heard the carriage that rattled toward them at great speed from the direction of Jermyn Street. She mounted hastily and had barely sat down when Samuel climbed up beside her. But he had no time to move the phaeton to the left side of the street before the other carriage was upon them.

The horses snorted and backed nervously. The oncoming pair, visible as huge dark shadows, reared as the other coachman pulled on the reins. His curses rent the air.

At the last moment, the approaching pair veered sharply, then came to a halt. The carriage, an open barouche, partially blocked the path of the phaeton.

In the feeble light of the flambeau, Sophy stared at the occupant of the barouche. The Lady in Gray.

"Madame Victoire," whispered Véronique.

The barouche started to move. Madame Victoire

raised a hand. There was a flash of silver—like a coin tossed carelessly, and yet quite unlike a coin.

As the barouche gathered speed and rattled off in the direction of St. James's Square, Sophy felt Véronique slump against her shoulder.

Instinctively, she put an arm around the other girl. "Véronique, are you unwell?"

"By George!" said Samuel. "If that weren't the same barouche as locked wheels with me in t' park. And the same one that stopped in Berkeley Square the night Lady Jane had her ball. I r'member it well. 'Twas around midnight, just when Mr. Andrew and some other young sprig arrived at Dolwyn House. Three times I've seen the veiled lady. What d'ye say, Miss Sophy? Does it mean good luck? Or bad?"

Sophy stared at the hilt of a silver dagger protruding from Véronique's chest.

"Samuel!" Her voice seemed detached from her body and mind, both numb and utterly useless. "Mademoiselle de Bouvier has been stabbed."

Twenty-two

Before Samuel Trueblood could say or do anything, two men, the same young blades who had whistled when Sophy and Véronique entered Louis's building, came running from the house across the street where Andrew had his chambers.

"Let me help, miss." The taller of the two, a freckle-faced man in an emerald velvet coat, reached for Véronique.

"Don't touch her!" Sophy said sharply.

She placed her fingers at the base of Véronique's throat and felt an almost imperceptible flutter of pulse.

Hope and fear hoarsened her voice. "Fetch a physician! Hurry!"

The second young man, as pudgy as his friend was lanky, stepped closer. "We're from the Admiralty, miss. We'll do all we can for the young lady."

"Fetch a physician! And if you're from the Admiralty, send for Lord Barham as well. And the barouche! One of you should be pursuing it. My coachman and I will carry Mademoiselle de Bouvier to Mr. Payne's chambers."

The men exchanged looks.

"Are you Miss Bancroft?" asked the stout one.

"I am, and if you have orders to stop me, let me remind you that so far you've made poor work of it."

"We also had orders not to interfere with Mademoiselle de Bouvier," said the tall, lanky man.

"I don't give a straw. Now, will you please do something constructive!"

Sophy heard a soft moan and bent close to Véronique. A whisper reached her ear. It sounded like "Bloomsbury."

"Shh, Véronique. Save your strength. You can tell me later."

"Sophy . . ."

"I'm here. Please don't worry about anything."

Her voice as soft as a breath, Véronique said, "Friends . . . ?"

"Yes, of course."

Sophy's throat tightened and she could say no more. She clasped Véronique's hand and pressed it.

There was no response.

"Véronique," she tried again. "I assure you, we are friends."

"Miss Sophy," Samuel Trueblood said gently. "Mamzelle is dead."

Sophy shook her head. Véronique could not be dead. Her face was relaxed, the mouth curved in a smile.

But the eyes, those dark, mysterious eyes were blank.

Through a blur of tears, Sophy looked at Samuel. He had removed his hat and held it against his chest.

She turned to the Admiralty men. They had taken a respectful step backward and they, too, had removed their hats.

But respect for the dead must wait. And so must mourning.

"The barouche!" Sophy said sharply. "You must have seen what happened. Don't just stand there. Go after it!"

The man in the emerald green coat shook his head. "Can't leave. Orders, miss. With your permission, we'll carry mademoiselle to Mr. Payne's rooms now. Better to get her out of the street, if you know what I mean."

Still holding Véronique's body in her arms, Sophy stared at him. She did not know what he meant; her mind was blanketed in a thick fog through which she must fight her way.

A third man—she had not even noticed when he joined the others—spoke in a paternal manner.

"I'm Marcus Wandsworth from the Admiralty, Miss Bancroft. You just let go now of Mademoiselle de Bouvier. You wouldn't want her cousin to stumble on this scene, would you now?"

Véronique's cousin. Louis. The name served to clear Sophy's mind.

She relinquished Véronique to the two young men, who carried her across the street toward Andrew's building. Sophy watched them disappear inside, then climbed down from the phaeton.

"Miss Sophy!" Samuel Trueblood said sternly. "Where d'ye think ye're goin'?"

Ignoring the coachman, Sophy turned to Marcus Wandsworth, a man in his late fifties or early sixties, soberly dressed in a brown coat and brown knee breeches.

"You're a senior clerk at the Admiralty, aren't you, Mr. Wandsworth? The clerk who is friends with the chief Bow Street Runner."

"Yes, Miss Bancroft. Like you, I'm interested in the detection of crime."

"Lucian was correct, then? In spite of Andrew's arrest, the Admiralty is still pursuing the possibility that Louis de Bouvier killed Peter Marston?"

"Quite correct. And Lord Barham has done me the honor of asking me to join the investigation force. The two young sprigs you met earlier have temporarily been quartered in Mr. Payne's rooms, which are ideal for the surveillance of anyone entering and leaving the building in which Monsieur de Bouvier resides."

"But one of them should have gone after the barouche! The veiled woman was Madame Victoire, to whom most of the Rye letters were addressed. Mademoiselle de Bouvier identified her."

The information did not ruffle Mr. Wandsworth's calm. "I know about the letters addressed to Madame Victoire. And I'm certain someone did pursue the barouche."

Beset by sudden doubts, Sophy hesitated. Marcus Wandsworth was one of the clerks. He had not been in the First Lord's outer office when Sir Jermyn handed over the Rye letters. But Simon Wandsworth, his son, was there. It would only be natural for a son to exchange a word or two with his father, wouldn't it?

"I'm afraid I cannot be as certain as you that someone went after the barouche," she said. "Who would it be? The two young gentlemen who saw what happened certainly did not."

"More men are stationed farther down the street. And since we've all been told about the veiled woman in St. Martin's Lane the night Lieutenant Marston's man was killed, someone will have followed this particular veiled lady."

The clock of St. James's church struck the hour of nine.

"Miss Sophy!" Samuel Trueblood's voice held a note of desperation. "We must get home! Ye're missing dinner. Whatever will Miss Addie think?"

Sophy felt a pang of remorse. Miss Addie had been kindness itself since her arrival at Payne House as the children's governess. The last thing she wanted to do was to cause worry for Miss Addie.

And Lucian—what would Lucian think if he returned from the Foreign Office and learned she had gone out to meet Véronique in Hyde Park? Skeet would surely tell him.

But she would gladly face Lucian's displeasure . . . if only he had returned. If only he were at Payne House when she arrived with the news of Véronique's death. She needed to feel his arms around her. She needed his comfort. She needed him.

"You go on home, Miss Bancroft," said Mr. Wandsworth. "There's nothing more you can do here. I'll see to it that Mademoiselle de Bouvier's parents are told in a proper and respectful manner."

Sophy looked up at Andrew's windows. Not a sliver of light showed. But, then, the men would not light a lamp that would betray their presence in one of the front rooms.

And Véronique—most likely, they had laid her down on the narrow couch in the back chamber.

Hastily, Sophy recalled her thoughts. She did not want to think about Véronique dead. Not now. But there was something she could do for Véronique and her parents. Immediately.

She studied Marcus Wandsworth, his upright, assured carriage, his calm face. The man inspired confidence.

"Mr. Wandsworth, Mademoiselle de Bouvier had nothing to do with her cousin's activities."

"Then what was her interest in Lieutenant Marston? I understand you were with her the morning she tried to enter his chambers."

"She was betrothed to Peter Marston. His death was a devastating blow. When I told her about Mr. Payne's arrest and mentioned the possibility that Louis de Bouvier killed Peter, she offered to help search her cousin's rooms for the driving coat the ostler identified as Andrew's, and for a blond wig."

Marcus Wandsworth was all attention. "And did you find the coat and wig?"

She hesitated, once more assailed by doubt. But she must place her trust in *someone*.

"We found them in the wardrobe of Monsieur de Bouvier's spare chamber."

"Knowing you consider yourself somewhat of an expert in the investigation of crime, I hesitate to ask. But ask I must. Where are the coat and wig now, Miss Bancroft?"

"Still in the wardrobe. Mademoiselle de Bouvier and I replaced everything exactly as we found it. I challenge you—or anyone—to discover a trace of our search."

"Thank you for telling me. I will immediately take appropriate measures." Marcus Wandsworth bowed. "It was a pleasure meeting you, Miss—"

He broke off to listen to the distant rattle of a carriage. When it was obvious that the vehicle, driven at a fast pace, was coming down York Street, he drew Sophy into the sheltered doorway of Andrew's building.

"The phaeton," said Sophy. "It's so very conspicuous in front of Louis's door."

"No more so than any gentleman's carriage in St. James's."

Sophy said no more, for the curricle swerving to avoid a collision with the phaeton was Kit Hawthorne's curricle. On the narrow tiger's perch at the rear of the vehicle stood Sedgewicke, clinging to the strap with both hands. And on the seat beside Kit sat Lucian.

The sight of him, so welcome, so dear, snapped the tight control Sophy kept on her emotions.

"Lucian!"

Picking up her skirts, she darted into the street. He had barely time to jump from the curricle and open his arms before she hurled herself against his chest.

"Lucian! Véronique is dead. Killed by Madame Victoire."

She buried her face against the cloth of his coat, for the tears could no longer be suppressed. But now it was all right to cry. Lucian was here. His arms, strong and comforting, sheltered her. The slight rocking motion of his body soothed her.

She heard Lucian talk with Marcus Wandsworth. Kit's and Sedgewicke's voices joined in. She heard Madame Victoire mentioned, and Louis, and Véronique. But she was not concerned with the men's conversation. She was only grateful that now she would not have to talk about the flash of silver in Madame Victoire's hand; about Véronique, slumped suddenly against her shoulder, then still and lifeless in her arms.

Véronique de Bouvier, escaped from the terror in France . . . she had wanted to cut a dash among the ladies of the *ton* and catch a wealthy husband. Instead, she had fallen in love with a penniless naval lieutenant.

Peter was killed before Véronique could teach him to love her. And Véronique was killed before she could find consolation in the children the Vicomte Marchand could give her.

The tears slowed as anger built. Madame Victoire had much to answer for.

With a resolute sniff, Sophy banished the last of the tears. She raised her face to Lucian.

"My poor love," he said, breaking off his talk with the other men. "I'm very sorry about Véronique. I wish I could have been with you sooner."

"You've helped. I'm quite all right now. Ready to go on with the work."

Lucian said nothing but swept her up in his arms. He nodded to Wandsworth, Sedgewicke, and Kit, then carried her to the phaeton.

"I'll drive Miss Sophy home," he told Samuel Trueblood. "Lord Christopher will take you up with him."

Samuel climbed down, Sophy was deposited on the high perch, and Lucian took his seat beside her. With a flick of the reins, he set the horses in motion.

Sophy gave him a sidelong look. It was dark and the street poorly lit, but she could not miss the tight set of his mouth.

"You're angry with me for meeting Véronique."

"No. I knew you'd meet her if she asked you," he said calmly. "I'm angry at myself for not taking adequate measures for your protection."

"*My* protection? But, Lucian! I am not in danger. I never was."

"Allow me to disagree."

Again Lucian flicked the reins, and the horses broke into a fast canter.

"It is obvious that Madame Victoire, whoever she or he may be, feels cornered," he said. "Else she wouldn't have taken such drastic measures as killing Véronique in front of witnesses."

"Do you believe Madame Victoire will now come after me because I was with Véronique?"

"I don't intend to wait and find out."

With barely a check, the phaeton swept into Piccadilly, all but deserted on a Sunday night.

"But, Lucian! You cannot expect me to remain hidden in my room until Madame Victoire is caught!"

"No, I wouldn't demand that of you," Lucian said quietly. "Tomorrow morning, I am sending you to Rose Manor with Jonathan."

Twenty-three

Sophy gave Lucian an incredulous look. "You're jesting!"

"I am not. I should have sent you to Rose Manor the night I learned of Peter's death."

Her hand gripped the side panel of the seat as she strove for calm.

"I'm not a child to be sent off at a whim, yet you speak as if I had no say in the matter."

"I should think you'd agree with me. The situation is entirely too dangerous."

"There's always an element of danger in the investigation of a crime. Gracious, Lucian! Surely you don't think that would frighten me."

"I don't. That's why you're leaving."

In the ominous silence following his words, Sophy's ears filled with the clatter of the horses' hooves and the rattle of the phaeton's wheels as they turned into Clarges Street. She saw Payne House ahead on the left, the steps and entrance lit by lanterns affixed above the wide arch of the door. A town carriage stood waiting in front of the house.

She thought of Andrew, imprisoned inside, falsely accused of treason and murder. And now she must tell him about Véronique, who had died helping to clear his name.

"Lucian, I'm *not* leaving."

He reined in, and the phaeton rolled to a stop behind the waiting carriage. The face he turned toward her was unutterably weary.

"Sophy, I've spent two harrowing nights and days in argument and negotiation with the Portuguese ambassador. I will not argue or negotiate with my betrothed."

"Dash it, Lucian—"

Sophy would have liked nothing better than to prove him wrong but was forced to bite her tongue when the front door of Payne House opened. A spectacled gentleman, followed by a liveried servant carrying a black leather case, came down the steps, doffed his hat, and bowed to her before entering the town carriage.

"Sir Alastair Block," said Lucian. "The physician sent by Lord Barham."

A footman had gone to the horses' heads, and Lucian climbed down. He went around to Sophy's side.

"I understand he came at your request?"

She thought she caught a hint of amusement in his voice, and said stiffly, *"Somebody* had to take the matter in hand, since Andrew refused to stay in bed."

"Sir Alastair was closeted with Andrew when I returned from the Foreign Office. I dare not speculate what illness the poor fellow suffers, that it would take over an hour to diagnose."

"Anything will be better than influenza."

Lucian gripped her waist and swung her down in

the masterful way that had so often set her heart racing. This time, it only served to annoy her.

"I am perfectly able to use the step!"

"I don't doubt it, but I like holding you."

"How can you speak and act as if you hadn't just ordered me off to Rose Manor! Lucian, we must talk. You cannot expect me to simply forget or, worse, to submit to your demand."

Lightly touching her elbow, he guided her toward the front steps. "You know me for a liberal man—how often you've called me a revolutionary! But there are some matters in which a woman must bow to the wishes of her betrothed or her husband. Especially when her safety is at stake."

Again, Sophy was forced to withhold comment unless she wanted to pull caps with Lucian in front of witnesses gathered in the entrance hall. Irritation and frustration roiled. If she must bottle up her feelings much longer, she would explode.

But beneath the irritation other, more disquieting feelings pushed to the surface. She knew Lucian as masterful, but never autocratic. Had he hidden that side of his nature? Or had she refused to see it?

There was no time to deal with doubts and uncertainties. Andrew, Miss Addie, and Jonathan claimed her and Lucian's attention as soon as they stepped across the threshold.

Andrew's voice was the most persistent, overpowering even Jonathan's disgruntled tones.

"Sophy, what the devil do you mean by setting that quack on me! Do you know what I'm supposed to suffer now? An *irritation of the nerves!* Like some vaporish, lachrymose female!"

A crack of laughter came from Lucian, but Sophy refused to see the funny side of the matter.

"My diagnosis would have been an inflammation of the brain. Dash it, Andrew! You ought to be grateful that you need no longer sneak out of your room."

"Indeed," said Miss Addie. "I worried when I found Jane in Andrew's study. Influenza is so very catching. But Andrew finally assured me that his illness was all a hum."

"It was Jane, the little feather-head, who blurted everything out," said Andrew with a guilty look at his brother.

Miss Addie nodded her silver-gray head. "Yes, but it was you who assured me that you were only acting a part. What was it you said? Ah, yes. A part in Lord Barham's game of intrigue." She smiled proudly. "To think that my nephews are playing a major role in the capture of a traitor!"

Sophy looked at Lucian. A game of intrigue? What a cork-brained thing to say. Andrew had outdone himself.

But what she read in Lucian's face and eyes confirmed his aunt's innocent disclosures.

Sophy's mind reeled. It was true, then. Andrew's arrest had, indeed, been part of a game.

And Lucian had known all along. He had lied to her. Slowly, she turned away from him. Hoping her movements didn't look as wooden as they felt, she walked toward the stairs.

"Lord Barham sent the wrong man to Wales. He should have kept Sir Jermyn in town and invented a family emergency for Andrew."

"Sophy!"

She heard Lucian's firm, quick tread behind her but neither turned nor stopped.

"Sophia Bancroft!" Jonathan's voice reverberated through the entrance hall. "How dare you walk off without a word after disappearing for hours on end! I want to know where you were."

She had reached the fifth step on the stairs. Gripping the banister, she swung around. She was momentarily disconcerted to find Lucian only a step or two behind her, but tore her gaze away from him and looked straight at her cousin.

"I went to see a killing, Jonathan. The murder of a young lady."

Sophy owed it to Miss Addie's interference that she had been allowed to escape to the third floor and turn the key in her door. Andrew and Jonathan had demanded explanations, but Miss Addie, with uncharacteristic sharpness, had ordered both men to "leave the poor girl be" and had steered them to Lucian with their questions.

But now it was morning, and a night of solitude had done no more for Sophy than save her from making a fool of herself by bursting into tears in front of three gentlemen.

She had lain sleepless most of the night. She had thought about Lucian and his work that demanded he lie to his betrothed. About his demand that she go to Rose Manor. And when she did fall asleep, she had dreamed uneasily of Véronique, of the flash of silver that had killed her. Sophy had woken with Véronique's last whispered words on her mind. Bloomsbury. Friends . . .

The Lady in Gray—Madame Victoire—had snuffed the friendship before it had fully bloomed.

A painful tightening in her chest warned Sophy that she must not dwell on that what might have been.

Bloomsbury, Véronique had whispered. Bloomsbury—where Peter Marston's widowed mother lived with two of her daughters. Where Peter had recuperated after the loss of his foot. Was it where Peter had spent time before he visited Andrew's chambers? Before he was killed?

Sophy wanted nothing more than to order the carriage for an immediate visit to Peter's mother, but it was the morning Lucian expected her to leave with Jonathan.

She looked around her chamber. She hadn't packed as much as a handkerchief.

Sophy went downstairs, hesitating on the first floor where Lucian had his study. He knew of her passion to solve crimes. He was aware of her sympathy and liking for Peter and Véronique. He certainly knew that, unlike most young ladies, she was not a biddable girl. He must know she wouldn't meekly drive off with Jonathan.

But did he?

She had believed she understood Lucian. She knew he felt responsible for her. She knew he was chivalrous and protective. Yet she had expected his support and had been utterly taken aback by his order to leave.

And the lie—

Purposefully, she went down the corridor on her right. If Lucian hadn't gone to the Foreign Office as usual, she might as well face him now. She opened the study door, and stopped on the threshold.

"You're home."

"Yes." Lucian turned from the window. "I was waiting for you."

"To see me off?"

Shutting the door, she leaned against the oaken panels. Now that she faced him, she felt woefully unprepared for a confrontation.

"Or did you want to explain Lord Barham's 'game of intrigue'?"

"Both."

Across the room, they measured each other. To Lucian, she had never looked more desirable. Or more unattainable. She was a slight woman, might even at the moment need the support of the door behind her, but the tilt of her head showed determination, and her eyes squarely met and held his.

"When I learned of Andrew's arrest," he said, "I was determined to fight the Board of Admiralty. Sir Jermyn supported me. Despite the evidence, his belief in Andrew's integrity remained unshaken. The rest of the Board was convinced they had caught the traitor."

He paused, half expecting a comment. But Sophy said nothing.

"After the meeting, Barham spoke privately to Andrew, Sir Jermyn, and me. He believed the evidence against Andrew, but he is a fair and painstakingly thorough man. He offered to continue the investigation if I stopped protesting Andrew's arrest. He—"

"He set a trap," Sophy interrupted. "With Andrew as bait."

"With Napoleon's forces gathered across the Channel, Barham cannot risk further betrayal."

"And he asked you to tell no one."

"Not even the members of the Board."

"Except for Sir Jermyn."

He could not tell what Sophy was thinking. Her face was expressionless, her voice bland. She still had not moved from the door, and he had the uncomfortable feeling she would walk out at the slightest provocation.

He said, "Sir Jermyn is fully cognizant of his weakness for gossip. You believed it a conspiracy that he left for Wales when, in truth, he wanted to remove himself and his loose tongue from town."

"I understand."

"Do you, Sophy? I assure you, it was not my wish to keep you in the dark. And in any case, there was not much I could have told you. Lord Barham made no promises regarding Andrew's release. If the traitor is not found . . ." He shrugged eloquently.

She pushed away from the door and took a few agitated steps toward him, but the feeling of distance between them was undiminished.

"My mind understands that there may always be matters you must keep secret, even when I have become your wife. But my heart—it wants to know everything you're doing, every bit of intrigue you're involved in.

"The same goes for me, Sophy. I tell myself I mustn't shackle your spirit of independence, your courage, your passion for investigation. Yet I want— like any other man—to know you safely at home. At the least, I want to be told *before* you go out on your own."

"I would have told you had you been here."

His voice was dry. "So *I* am to blame when you set

out to do what a trained agent would hesitate to undertake."

"Searching Louis's apartment? There was no danger, Lucian. And even if he had been home, Véronique and I would have found a way to look for Andrew's coat."

"I never doubted your ingenuity."

If she suspected sarcasm, she did not show it.

"And I didn't mean to cast blame or to reproach you, Lucian. Your duty lies with the Foreign Office." She drew an unsteady breath. "I am willing to accept secrecy. Even a lie. I am willing to accept that I mustn't expect you to dance attendance on me day and night."

"And in turn, I suppose, you want my assurance that I'm willing to allow you to go your way. Without let or hindrance."

"Precisely."

"Dammit, Sophy! I cannot do that."

He crossed the room in a few long strides. She did not move, yet he gripped her shoulders as if he must stop her from running away.

"I love you, Sophy. More than life itself. When I arrived in York Street yesterday and Wandsworth told me about Véronique, I gave thanks it wasn't you lying lifeless in Andrew's chambers. But how easily it could have been you!"

"I understand. Truly, I do! Do you think I'm not afraid when you are sent abroad? The time you went to Courland to see King Louis—do you think I did not tremble at the thought of your crossing war-torn Germany?"

"I had an escort, and we were armed. But you—" He crushed her to his breast. "Sophy, I couldn't bear losing you!"

She wound her arms around his waist and held him, as he held her—tightly, possessively.

She did understand. But understanding Lucian's feelings did not change her own.

Gently, she drew apart.

"Lucian, this is not merely about your ordering me off with Jonathan so I won't be hurt by Madame Victoire. This is about our future life. I don't doubt you'll be given an ambassadorship before long. But, understandably, it will be a post in a minor, possibly remote country at first."

"Yes," he said wryly. "It'll hardly be Lisbon or St. Petersburg, or Paris once we've beaten Bonaparte. But that's not what bothers you, is it?"

"I fear that wherever we'll be, you will demand that I stay within the safety of the embassy. That I don't venture out without you or an armed escort."

He did not say anything, only looked at her very intently.

Her heart pounded painfully fast. "Lucian, I know I should not feel this way. But I fear that you will stifle me with your protectiveness."

Twenty-four

A taut white groove appeared at the corner of Lucian's mouth.

"Harsh words, Sophy. But let us, for the present, stay with the subject at hand. The Admiralty investigation."

"By all means let us do so. We're destined to move in government circles, and there will always be intrigue and mystery to draw me like a lode stone. There will always be someone to whom I take a liking and who will need my help."

He looked into her eyes, and wished he did not have to say the words that would dull the clear, frank gaze.

"Sophy, this involves more than my fear for your safety." His voice softened. "Don't you see? With your visit to Louis's chambers you not only forced Madame Victoire's hand but also forced the Admiralty investigators to arrest Louis de Bouvier prematurely."

She blanched. "Are you saying Véronique would be alive if we had not gone to York Street?"

"No!" He cradled her face with his hands. "You are not to blame for her death. Véronique forfeited her life when she requested the meeting."

"Then what do you mean? You said I forced Madame Victoire's hand."

His hands dropped away from her face, but the warmth of his touch lingered comfortingly.

"After killing Véronique, Madame Victoire tried to kill Louis. Fortunately, the dagger only scraped his arm because one of the men shadowing him knocked him down."

"I wish it had been Véronique who was fortunate."

"Yes, indeed. But I meant it was fortunate for the Admiralty agents. They cannot interrogate a dead man."

"So they arrested him," she said dryly. "May I ask why the arrest is considered premature?"

"Because we did not gain much with the arrest. We have Louis's walking stick, which does hide a sword, but we have no identification of Madame Victoire. Louis swears he never saw her without the veil."

"And Madame Victoire, I daresay, got away once more."

"She did." Lucian's fingers drummed a silent beat on the desk top. "The Admiralty men got a good look at her. She fits the description of—"

"Of the veiled lady in Peter Marston's lodging house," Sophy cut in. "The night his servant was stabbed. Clearly, it was Madame Victoire who killed him, and clearly, it was she who left Peter's rooms in shambles when she was searching them for—oh, whatever! Which proves that Peter was not involved in treasonous activities, doesn't it?"

"I'm afraid not."

"Dash it, Lucian! You cannot have paid attention to what I said. Clearly—"

"Sophy, we found the dispatches sent by Admiral

Nelson in Louis's coat pocket. And Lord Barham's reply to Nelson."

"The papers Louis took from Peter, after he killed him!" A gleam lit in Sophy's eye. "Which proves—"

"Which proves that Peter removed the documents from the Admiralty. And that he had started to copy them. Besides the originals, the agents also found a duplicate set of the Nelson dispatches in Louis's pockets. Duplicates written in Peter's hand."

Sophy was silenced.

"It proves," Lucian continued relentlessly, "that Peter was one of the men who, time after time, betrayed the crown."

Sophy started to pace.

"Will anyone ever understand the male brain? So logical. So precise." She whirled to face him. "So easily misled by appearances."

"And the female brain!" he shot back. "So easily ruled by the heart."

"Which is why the two must work together."

"Not in this case. Sophy—"

Whatever else Lucian might have said remained unspoken. A knock fell on the door and Horace poked his head into the room.

"Lord Barham arrived, my lord. I just took him to Mr. Andrew's study."

Without taking his eyes off Sophy, Lucian said, "Tell Lord Barham I'll join them shortly."

"Go now." She swallowed. It had not been easy to say she was willing to play second fiddle to the government; it was even more difficult to *do*. "We can talk later."

"I appreciate your forbearance." Lucian's voice and look were strained. "I shall see you at Rose Manor as soon as the situation permits."

"No, Lucian. We shall speak *here*. When you have the time."

She stepped past him and went quickly to the door where Horace still lingered.

"Post has come, Miss Sophy. A letter for Miss Addie and one for you."

"Thank you." She accepted her letter absently. "You'll find Miss Addie in her rooms."

Lucian touched her arm. "I'm afraid there won't be time to talk before you leave. Jonathan's chaise will be at the door in an hour."

"I shall be glad to see the last of him."

Ignoring the thunder cloud on Lucian's brow, she followed Horace's solid form retreating down the corridor. Behind her, she heard a door open and Andrew hailing his brother.

"Lucian, old boy! Hurry up, will you? Lord Barham has news—albeit not what we expected."

Sophy slowed her step, but the door closed and she heard no more. She was tempted to go back, but the First Lord's news must wait. She had other important business to tend. And, for once, Jonathan and his predilection for gambling would be of use to her.

She continued down the corridor, quiet now, save for Horace's heavy tread on the stairs as he continued to the second floor with the other letter.

Her gaze fell on the letter he had handed her. It was addressed to Miss Adelaide Payne. Pensive, she stared at the inscription.

Adelaide Payne. Sophia Bancroft. The names could not possibly be confused or misread.

But even a serious talk with Horace must wait.

* * *

Having placed Miss Addie's letter on the hall table, Sophy ordered the carriage for a drive to Bloomsbury, then entered the breakfast parlor where, the footman had told her, she would find Lord Wingfield.

"Jonathan, I cannot possibly be ready in an hour."

He was in the process of carving slices of beefsteak at the sideboard and did not look up from the task.

"Dammit, Sophia! It's you and your madcap starts that put Northrop in queer stirrups and made him decide you must go to Rose Manor. The least you can do is get ready on time."

"You don't want to leave town, do you, Jonathan?"

He served himself three juicy slices of the beef. "What I want is of no account."

Sophy blinked at this uncharacteristic show of selflessness and interpreted it as a sign that Lucian had bribed or coerced Jonathan into cooperation.

"I'll need at least three hours to pack," she said.

"Three hours!" His color and temper rose but ebbed when his eye fell on the long-case clock behind Sophy. "When a woman says three hours, she means four. It'll be too late to start out then."

Sophy said nothing.

"Where's Northrop?" asked Jonathan.

"Upstairs, closeted with Andrew and someone from the Admiralty."

"Tell you what." Jonathan set down his plate among the chafing dishes. "If you're done packing by eleven, we'll leave today. If not—"

He shrugged and started for the door as fast as his bulk allowed.

"Where will you be, Jonathan?"

"At White's."

Sophy suppressed a smile. At White's he would be out of Lucian's way, an arrangement that suited her as well as it did Jonathan.

As she left the dining room, the front door shut with a slam—the typical Jonathan touch.

Miss Addie's letter on the hall table had been replaced with a letter addressed to Miss Sophia Bancroft in an elegant copperplate, which Sophy had no trouble recognizing as her sister Linnet's.

She slid open the seal and unfolded the stiff vellum. Linnet wrote that she was leaving Bath immediately, would most likely already be at Rose Manor when Sophy read the note. Linnet expected it would take a day or two to convince Cousin Jonathan that Caro and Susannah should accompany her to London, and then—

Sophy read no more. She hardly knew whether to laugh or cry. Since Jonathan was *not* at Rose Manor, her sisters and Susannah might already be on their way to town.

She heard the carriage pull up at the door and hurried outside. Not Lucian, not Jonathan or the pending arrival of Linnet and Caro must delay an interview with Peter Marston's mother.

Sophy was not surprised to see the groom, Mel, climb down from the seat beside Samuel Trueblood and open the carriage door for her. Bloomsbury was a goodly drive, and long stretches of the road were nothing more than rough country lane. One never knew when a second man would be needed to fetch a wheelwright or to hold the horses if one of them caught a pebble in his shoe. But she was utterly taken aback to see Mel with a blunderbuss clutched under his arm.

"Great heavens! Put that gun away before you shoot yourself in the foot."

"Mr. Trueblood's orders, Miss Sophy. I'm not to let it out o' me hand."

Sophy brushed past Mel. Scowling, she looked up at the coachman on the box.

"What is this nonsense, Samuel? There are no highwaymen on the way to Bloomsbury."

"Who says anything about the high toby? It's the veiled lady I'm thinkin' of. Ain't about to let her close enough so she can throw her dagger at you, Miss Sophy."

"Rubbish," said Sophy, but her voice lacked conviction.

First Lucian, now Samuel showed concern. And she could not deny that Madame Victoire had seen her with Véronique. Twice.

Turning, she said, "At least hide the dratted thing."

Mel was not called upon to fire the blunderbuss during the drive to Bloomsbury or when they stopped in Tavistock Square, where the Widow Marston resided with two of her daughters.

Tavistock was one of the older squares, built—along with Russell, Torrington, Woburn, and Gordon Squares—soon after the development of the Bedford estate and the removal of the Duke of Bedford's household from Covent Garden to the new mansion in quiet Bloomsbury. All around, lesser estates were still being developed, the streets already paved and the squares neatly laid out but as yet bare of buildings.

As she approached Mrs. Marston's front door accented with keystones and brickwork, Sophy faltered at the sight of black crepe draped around the knocker. Usually an intrepid soul, she was tempted to turn back to the carriage, to tell Samuel Trueblood to drive on. That she hadn't wanted to stop in Tavistock Square at all but wanted to see the Bedford Gardens farther on or, perhaps, take a spin through Hampstead Heath, a short distance off.

But, of course, Sophy went on. She was thrusting herself into a house of mourning. She was intruding upon a mother's grief. But, if the Admiralty had its way, to Mrs. Marston's grief would soon be added shame. And that Sophy would do her best to prevent. Peter was dead, but his reputation should live. Unblemished.

Twenty-five

A half hour later, clutching two letters in her hand, Sophy climbed back into the carriage.

"Home, Mel. And please ask Samuel to hurry. I carry important news for Mr. Andrew and the Admiralty."

But, as usual, Samuel Trueblood had his own notion of "hurry." In his estimation, a lady of quality must be conveyed with dignity and not as though she were rushing off to an elopement.

As they rolled toward Russell Square, Sophy once more skimmed Peter Marston's messages to Andrew and to Véronique. She had no compunction about doing so. The seals had been broken earlier that morning by Peter's mother.

Andrew's letter posed no problem. She would deliver it. But what to do with Véronique's?

It was dated Wednesday, the third day of July, seven o'clock. The night Peter was killed. The salutation read simply, *Véronique.*

Our last meeting weighs heavy on my mind. I assure you that, no matter what my intention was originally, I no longer wish to break the betrothal once I come into the inheritance.

Véronique, I have learned to respect and admire you,

*and when I return from Bournemouth, I shall speak to
your father. We will use the inheritance to buy a small
property far away from Louis and Madame Victoire.*
   Yours,
   Peter

The boldly penned words blurred. Hastily, Sophy
folded the letter and tucked it into her reticule.

In the note to Andrew, Peter mentioned that he
was followed, but that he had shaken off the pursuer long before Bloomsbury. Peter intended to go
to Dolwyn House to speak to Lord Barham and to
Véronique. He did not think he was in danger of
his life—not until dawn when he would set out for
Bournemouth. However, as a precaution, he would
deposit the orders for Admiral Calder with Andrew
in York Street until it was time to fetch the hack
from the livery stable.

And just in case he did not make it to Dolwyn
House, Peter left the note for Véronique and the letter for Andrew in a safe place at his mother's home.
A safe place, indeed; the letters had not been discovered until that morning, five days after Peter's death.

Sophy slid Andrew's letter beside Véronique's in
the reticule.

She could not help but wonder if Véronique
would be alive if the messages had been discovered
sooner. In the note to Andrew, Peter explained his
involvement with Louis de Bouvier and with
Madame Victoire. Like Louis, Peter swore he did
not know the identity of Madame Victoire. But on
one occasion, he had heard the head of French
agents speak above the usual whisper. The voice was
that of a man. An Englishman.

Sophy stifled a sigh. What a poor investigator she made. Bit by bit, she had been handed clues that— had she not been preoccupied with tangential events—should have led her to the identity of the traitor.

She had allowed herself to be ruled by emotion. To her, it had been more important to prove that Peter and Andrew were *not* traitors than to discover who *was* the traitor. It had been more important to find Peter's and Véronique's killers than to discover the mastermind behind the treason plot.

She should have remembered Peter's mother and sisters the moment she realized that the last four hours of Peter's life—from six o'clock, when he left Whitehall, until Horace admitted him to Andrew's chambers in York Street—were unaccounted for.

The day she learned of Andrew's arrest, she should have proceeded to the Admiralty as planned instead of badgering the ostler at Brompton's Livery Stables in a fruitless interview. At the Admiralty, she would have made the acquaintance of the clerks.

She should have talked with Horace again, and she should have made an effort to see Sir Jermyn and Lord Dolwyn. She should have—

A jerk of the carriage as it suddenly picked up speed thrust her against the squabs.

She straightened, clinging to the strap suspended from the roof, and with some difficulty transferred to the seat back-to-back with the coachman's box. A look out the window showed they were careening along one of the streets under development.

She opened the small panel that allowed her to communicate with the coachman. "Samuel! What is going on?"

It was Mel who answered, his voice all but lost in the rumble of wheels and the drumbeat of hooves.

"Mr. Trueblood says there's the veiled lady behind us. He says not to worry. We'll be in Russell Square in no time at all."

Excitement flared. "I'm not worried. But we must stop her! Tell Samuel to slow down. Block the street. Anything. Just stop her!"

"Don't want to brangle with a French spy, Miss Sophy!" shouted Mel. "Not until we got you safe!"

"Balderdash!" she shouted back. "Stop her, I say! It's an order!"

For a moment she heard nothing but the rattle of the carriage.

Then, Samuel's voice. "Beggin' yer pardon, Miss Sophy, but I've had me orders from Lord Northrop. And I ain't stoppin' for nothing till we gets to Russell Square."

"The deuce!" she said, forgetting for once that a lady did not swear.

Twisting in the seat, she tried to look through the open panel without losing her grip on the strap. But, of course, there was nothing to see but the backs of two pairs of boots.

Sophy snapped the panel shut. She had no intention of shouting herself hoarse when she knew argument was futile.

Samuel Trueblood would no more disobey Lucian's orders than she would disregard the commands of her conscience.

The carriage rocked alarmingly. Her arm and hand grew numb as she clung to the strap. She did not much enjoy riding with her back to the horses, but it was preferable to being tossed about in the attempt to change seats again.

Perhaps they would overturn, she thought grimly, and she would end up with a broken neck. Then, what would Lucian think of his measures to protect her from Madame Victoire?

And where was the elusive lady? Still behind them? If only the carriage had a rear window so she could see for herself. Despite Lucian's warning, Sophy had only half believed the head of French agents would pursue her because of her friendship with Véronique.

She peeked out the window on her left but saw only a formal garden. On her right, stately houses flew by. Russell Square?

They took the turn around the garden at a reckless speed. Then, finally, the carriage slowed to what Sophy considered a manageable pace.

She heard Samuel shout something from the box. A stopped coach came into view on her right, a coach with a crest of strawberry leaves and the coat of arms of the dukes of Wigmore. The dowager duchess, she remembered, lived in Russell Square.

And just as she thought they would pull up, she heard the crack of Samuel's whip, and the carriage gathered speed once more. She caught a glimpse of the duchess's young coachman, who seemed to be shouting back at Samuel, but the words were lost in the clatter of hooves and wheels.

They rattled on, leaving Russell Square behind and traveling, if she was not mistaken, in the same direction from which they had just come.

She thrust open the panel. "Mel! Where are we going? Have we lost the veiled lady?"

"No, Miss Sophy! She's behind us."

"Then, where are we going?"

"Some quiet, undeveloped street, Miss Sophy. Mr. Trueblood got a notion to catch the spy!"

"Bless him," she said, surprised.

The rumble of wheels grew louder, the drumbeat of hooves more urgent. It sounded like a cavalcade of carriages giving each other chase.

Mel shouted something else, but Sophy understood only a few words, a reference to the Dowager Duchess of Wigmore's coachman. Was he following as well?

If only she were up on the box with Samuel and the groom. Inside the carriage, she felt blindfolded, useless, helpless.

A postilion's horn blasted shrilly behind them, answered immediately by a loud boom from the carriage box.

The blunderbuss, thought Sophy as a violent jerk loosened her grip on the strap and she was tossed into the seat corner.

"Mel!" she screamed. "What happened?"

There was no reply, only a scraping noise along the off-side of the carriage. Then they jolted to a stop.

Hastily, she straightened. They had hit something. Or something had hit them. But, at least, they hadn't overturned.

She cast a quick look out the window. They were indeed in a wide-open, undeveloped section of Bloomsbury. A barouche, its top folded back, had pulled up next to the carriage, so close that wheel touched wheel.

Holding the nervous horses in check with one hand, the driver of the barouche pointed a long-nosed pistol at the carriage or, rather, at Samuel and Mel. And trying to swing himself up the back of the barouche was the Dowager Duchess of Wig-more's coachman.

But there was no sign of Madame Victoire.

Sophy whirled. She thrust open the opposite door and, without bothering to let down the steps, jumped to the ground.

"Good morning, Miss Bancroft."

Low, insinuating, the voice drifted from beneath the veil as Madame Victoire stepped around the open door.

Sophy stood motionless. She paid no heed to the voice or to the words. Her attention centered on the silver dagger in Madame Victoire's right hand and on the need to stay calm, to betray no fear.

The point of the dagger rose.

"Miss Bancroft, may I trouble you for the letters you fetched from Tavistock Square?"

Her breath caught. "Damn you! If you harmed Mrs. Marston or her daughters—"

"You insult me. They can do *me* no harm, so what possible reason would I have to harm *them?*" Still speaking in an almost-whisper, the head of French agents took a step closer. "The letters. Please."

The drawstring cut into her wrist as she tightened her grip on the top of the reticule. She could not—*would* not—hand over the letters. They were needed to clear Peter Marston's reputation.

"The letters, Miss Bancroft!"

Gone was the softness, the insinuation. It was a man's voice. Impatient. Irritable. An Englishman's voice.

Just as Peter stated in his message to Andrew.

"Mel!" she screamed. "Fire the blunderbuss!"

Twenty-six

It was the pistol in the hand of Madame Victoire's driver that went off when he was thrust off the barouche by Will Ellison, the Dowager Duchess of Wigmore's coachman. The same coachman who on the night of the Dolwyn ball had shocked his colleagues by saying he wouldn't mind if the Emperor Napoleon rewarded him with a coaching inn in return for a bit of assistance with the invasion.

The ball buried itself harmlessly in a mound of dirt at the roadside, but the noise of the repercussion startled the horses.

The carriage behind Sophy rocked. The open door swung, flinging her to the ground and out of reach of the viciously thrusting dagger. Then Mel was there and knocked the dagger from Madame Victoire's hand with the stock of the blunderbuss.

Sophy was unhurt but stunned. She heard the rattle of wheels and thought at first that the pair harnessed to the barouche had bolted. But the rumble and thunder came closer, and the ground beneath her trembled.

Not one, but several vehicles were approaching

at great speed. She heard shouts and curses. Then, suddenly, quiet.

Relative quiet. Horses snorted, whickered, and stomped. There was a babel of voices. Dozens, it seemed. One voice raised above the others brought her scrambling to her feet.

"Sophy!"

She saw Sedgewicke, Horace, and Marcus Wandsworth, each armed with a pistol, surrounding Madame Victoire. Mel held the silver dagger.

"Sophy! Dammit, Samuel! If she's hurt, I'll have your hide."

Shaking the dust from her skirts, Sophy turned toward the voice. Her heart was beating disconcertingly fast.

"Sophy!" Lucian shouted again.

He rounded the carriage and stopped in his tracks when he saw her.

"Hello, Lucian." Hiding trepidation with an air of nonchalance, she started toward him. "Peter was *not* a traitor. He was killed because Madame Victoire found out that he led the French by their noses."

Lucian said nothing, and neither did he move.

Lord Barham, followed by Andrew, Jane, and Kit, came around the coach,

"Dash it, Sophy!" said Andrew. He was pale, and there was not a sign of the boyish grin that was so much a part of him. "You gave us quite a scare. Are you all right?"

"I'm fine." Sophy tugged at the strings of her reticule. "I have Peter's explanation of his involvement with Louis de Bouvier and Madame Victoire. He did give them information, but it was always falsified to mislead the French."

She handed Peter's letters to the First Lord.

"Madame Victoire never quite trusted Peter, and that's why she wanted him to marry Mademoiselle de Bouvier. Family ties, and all that. The letter also explains the papers Louis had in his pocket when he was arrested—the original dispatches from Admiral Nelson and Lord Barham's reply stolen from Lord Dolwyn's office, and the duplicate set of Nelson's dispatches in Peter's handwriting."

She was very much aware of Lucian, unmoving and silent, beside Lord Barham.

The words tumbled from her mouth. "Peter did copy the dispatches and planned to give them to Louis. Without Lord Barham's reply, of course, so the French would believe we're unaware of Villeneuve's movements. But Peter did not steal the originals. They disappeared from Lord Dolwyn's office *after* he told Louis what he had copied."

Lord Barham frowned at the letters. "You found these in Tavistock Square? My men thoroughly searched Peter's room when I informed Mrs. Marston of her son's tragic death. I don't see how they could have missed these."

"They were in Mrs. Marston's needlework basket. This morning was the first time she felt well enough to take out her embroidery."

"Can't say I blame her," said Andrew. "I haven't felt like doing anything since—"

He broke off and shot a grim look at the veiled figure standing between Sedgewicke and Marcus Wandsworth.

Jane touched his arm. "Mademoiselle de Bouvier's death will not go unpunished." Hesitantly, she added, "I admire her for her courage."

Andrew looked at Jane, and some of the grimness left his face. "Yes, she had courage. She must have known that Madame Victoire would kill anyone who betrayed their operation."

Lord Barham had skimmed the letters and handed Sophy the note addressed to Véronique. "Dispose of it as you see fit, Miss Bancroft. It is of no possible concern to the Admiralty."

He passed the other note to Andrew. "This confirms what we learned this morning from de Bouvier and his valet."

Her gaze on Lucian, who had joined Andrew and Kit for a look at the letter, Sophy asked, "Did Louis admit that he killed Peter?"

"He did," said Lord Barham. "But not until we took him to his chambers and confronted him with the driving coat and the wig. And we already had the sword stick. His valet, a timid man who wants only to return to France, admitted following Peter when he left Whitehall but lost track of him in Charing Cross."

"If Peter hadn't gone to York Street—"

"Yes, Miss Bancroft. It was mere chance that Louis de Bouvier was adjusting the drapes when Peter entered Andrew's building. The limp, unfortunately, made him conspicuous."

"Devil a bit!" said Andrew, who had finished reading Peter's letter. "Madame Victoire an Englishman!"

"In which case," said Kit, "we've caught not only the head of French agents but our spy as well."

Sophy was about to speak when Lord Barham ordered Sedgewicke to remove Madame Victoire's hat.

The hat and veil came off with a flourish, exposing a narrow face with prominent cheekbones, a tight mouth and long chin, and thinning hair of indeterminable color.

"By George!" said the First Lord.

"Well?" Sophy said impatiently when no one uttered the name she wanted to hear. "Is it Nolan Ashby?"

She glanced at Lucian, who nodded, then turned away to speak in an undertone to Andrew and Kit.

A heaviness settled on her. If only he would shake her. His silence was nigh impossible to bear.

"Why, Ashby?" asked Lord Barham. "You're the last man I would have suspected."

"*Why?*" Ashby's eyes blazed. His voice rasped, as if he had spoken in whispers too long. "Because I'm tired of being a clerk. I'm tired of getting shoved from office to office. I'm tired of bowing and scraping, of saying yes, my lord and no, my lord. I want to be a man of rank!"

"You'll get your rank," Andrew said coldly. "Highest rank among the gallows-birds."

Beneath the voluminous cloak, Ashby's chest puffed out. "I'll be Lord Mayor when the emperor's troops land. I have it in writing. Signed by Napoleon himself!"

"Poppycock!" said Kit. "You cannot mean that you paid attention to those blasted pamphlets!"

"Last year I wrote to the emperor. And he sent a letter back. Sealed and signed."

The blazing eyes shifted back to the First Lord of Admiralty. "And I tell you, my lord Barham, you'll rue this day! When I am in power, I'll have you and the bumbling members of the Admiralty Board arrested. And the interfering Miss Bancroft will suffer the fate of her friend, the foolish Mademoiselle de Bouvier."

The abrasive tone of Ashby's voice made Sophy shiver. She was glad he did not look at her; she would have hated it had he seen her weakness.

Then Lucian's hand cupped her shoulder, and the shivers ceased.

"Take him away," Lord Barham said curtly. "The traitorous fool."

Twenty-seven

"Sophy, how on earth did you figure out that it was Papa's clerk?" asked Jane. "You don't even know the man."

The Wigmore coach and the Admiralty carriages with the exception of Lord Barham's coach had departed, and Kit was trying to steer his sister toward the curricle. But Jane stood her ground beside Sophy.

Andrew was about to join Horace in the phaeton. At Jane's words he turned.

"Don't tell her, Sophy," he said. "Not unless you want to go over all the questions again when I get home. And no matter how clever you were in tracing the traitor, I still don't believe that Peter could open *my* safe to deposit the orders for Calder."

"Andrew," said Lord Barham, "forget about the bloody safe."

Lucian said, "I believe Sophy may have the answer to the puzzle."

He was looking straight at her, his expression inscrutable.

"Perhaps." She turned to Horace. "What do you say, Horace?"

He colored painfully. "I must've done it. I always put away papers with the Admiralty seal before I go out. And if the lieutenant left 'em on the desk, I would've grabbed 'em along with the others Mr. Andrew forgot to put away."

Andrew exploded. "The devil you say! You swore you didn't see the orders for Calder on my desk! Miss Sophy asked you. And, devil a bit, I asked you myself!"

"I cannot read, Mr. Andrew."

"*Not* read? But—" Andrew took a deep breath. "But you were helping the clerks when they turned Lieutenant Marston's office upside-down for the missing papers."

"That's what misled me, too," said Sophy. "But you judge papers by their seals, don't you, Horace?"

"Aye. If I had found a paper with the First Lord's seal in an open file in the outer office, I'd have known it don't belong there."

For a moment Andrew looked stunned. Then he gave a crack of laughter and quickly swung himself into the phaeton.

"I had better take Horace away before he confesses some other foolishness in front of the First Lord. Jane, I will see you later, won't I?"

"Yes, of course," replied Jane, blushing softly.

"Come along, Janey." Kit firmly gripped his sister's arm. "Father will want to hear the news."

"In a moment." Pulling against Kit's grip, Jane whispered into Sophy's ear, "Did you notice? Andrew no longer treats me as if I were his little niece."

"I noticed," Sophy whispered back. "Just don't get impatient."

"Oh, I won't. I'll give him at least a week to get over his tendre for Mademoiselle de Bouvier."

Finally giving in to the tug on her arm, Jane departed in her brother's wake and allowed him to hand her into the curricle.

Lord Barham turned to Sophy. "I owe you an apology, Miss Bancroft. None of us had figured out that Madame Victoire was Nolan Ashby. You are indeed, as Lucian assured me, an excellent investigator."

She gave Lucian a look of astonishment.

"I never denied your powers of deduction," he said.

"Thank you. But in this case, I'm afraid, I can take no credit as an investigator. I failed miserably."

"Nonsense," said Lord Barham.

Sophy shook her head. "I helped prove that Louis de Bouvier killed Peter. And I found Peter's letters." A rueful smile tugged at her mouth. "Which, had I not gone to Tavistock Square, would have been sent to the Admiralty this afternoon. But I did not follow the clues that would have led me to the traitor."

"Nolan Ashby—"

"He is Madame Victoire, the head of French agents. But is he the only traitor?"

Lucian and Lord Barham exchanged looks.

Sophy said, "I knew Nolan Ashby had been demoted from the First Lord's office to Lord Dolwyn's. The Nelson dispatches disappeared when Lord Dolwyn had them in his office for review. I knew that Ashby heard Sir Jermyn explain the Rye letters to Andrew, and he saw Andrew pass them to Horace. Admittedly, others did, too. But Horace let drop one other bit of information about Ashby. That he had ambitions to be 'alderman or something.'"

"Lord Mayor," Lord Barham muttered. "I see

how that would give you pause. Not too many clerks are chosen as alderman."

"No, it is usually a merchant of some standing, a master craftsman, a physician. But when I read in Peter's letter that Madame Victoire is an Englishman, I remembered the French pamphlets promising rank and riches. And I saw Ashby's ambition in a different light."

Lord Barham looked toward the carriages. Having assured himself that his coachman had joined Samuel Trueblood and Mel by the roadside for a friendly exchange of news and tobacco, he once more faced Sophy.

"You questioned whether Ashby is the *only* traitor."

"Yes, sir. Even the highest-ranking clerk does not have access to some of the information that leaked from the Admiralty. I submit that a member of the Board is guilty of treason."

With a weary shrug, the First Lord turned toward his carriage. "Northrop, take over."

"It started quite accidentally."

"The loose tongue?"

Lucian, with his back to the horses, sat stiffly opposite Sophy as Samuel Trueblood drove them home at a decorous pace.

He nodded. "That, and a tendency to boast when in the company of young ladies."

"Véronique said many Englishmen have that tendency." Sophy wondered how much longer Lucian would keep his distance and how much longer they would discuss a subject in which she had suddenly lost all interest. "I suppose one of the young ladies was in the pay of the French and reported him to Madame Victoire as a prospect for blackmail."

"Yes, but it wasn't Mademoiselle de Bouvier," he said, answering her unspoken question. Wanting to be done with the unpleasant subject, he hurried on. "It was a French courtesan, skillful in the art of subtle interrogation. And Nolan Ashby as Madame Victoire did the rest."

"Giving him the option to keep supplying information, or to have his name publicly disgraced."

Her hands clenched, and she realized she still held the letter from Peter to Véronique, the letter Lord Barham had told her to dispose of as she wished.

"Lucian, why do I feel sorry for him?"

"Because even villains can be likable."

"What will happen to him?"

"It has already happened. A courier arrived from Wales with news of a tragic accident. While cleaning his dueling pistols . . ."

Sophy sighed. "Poor Sir Jermyn."

Only the rattle of the carriage eased the sudden silence between them.

"What do you propose to do with the letter to Véronique?" asked Lucian, looking at her hand.

"I'll keep it. To remind me of the fragility of life and happiness."

Again, silence fell between them. Then, both started to speak at the same time and broke off at the same time. Sophy was the first to try again.

"Lucian, I *had* to do this. Just before she died, Véronique said something about Bloomsbury, but I did not see the significance until this morning. When I did, I knew I must see Peter's mother and ask her if he talked about his activities or if he left letters. You were so certain he was a traitor, and I—"

He moved with the speed of lightning, switching to the seat beside her. He crushed her to his breast. The next moment, she was thrust at arm's length for a thorough shaking, then once again caught in a crushing embrace.

"Dammit, Sophy! I could *throttle* you."

She peeked up at him. "I was hoping you'd shake me."

He looked at her intently.

"Are you certain?" His eyes darkened. "You aren't afraid any more that I will stifle you with my protectiveness? You aren't about to end our betrothal?"

She held quite still in his arms.

"Lucian, if we end the betrothal, it won't be at my instigation. I want nothing more than to get married as soon as possible, but I can never promise to make you a biddable wife. If that's what you want—"

Ruthlessly, he interrupted her. "I want *you*. I also want the privilege of being your protector. If you fight me on that point, I'll fight back. Can you live with that, Sophy?"

Her fingers tightened on Peter's letter to Véronique before she allowed it to drop onto the seat. She wound her arms around Lucian's neck.

"A Bancroft of Rose Manor can face anything."

"Anything? Even Jonathan for a month or so?"

"Lucian, don't tease." Her eyes widened. "You're not teasing. It's Susannah. And Linnet and Caroline. But, surely, they cannot have arrived yet?"

"Susannah sent a messenger. They'll be in town day after tomorrow."

"In that case, I can bear Jonathan, too." She smiled mischievously. "I'll use the opportunity to make him agree to an early wedding."

Then she could say no more. Lucian pulled her onto his lap and sealed her mouth with kisses that lasted from Russell Square to Clarges Street. And for once, Sophy did not find fault with Samuel Trueblood, who knew what pace befitted Viscount Northrop and his future bride.

BOOK YOUR PLACE ON OUR WEBSITE AND MAKE THE READING CONNECTION!

We've created a customized website just for our very special readers, where you can get the inside scoop on everything that's going on with Zebra, Pinnacle and Kensington books.

When you come online, you'll have the exciting opportunity to:

- View covers of upcoming books

- Read sample chapters

- Learn about our future publishing schedule (listed by publication month *and author*)

- Find out when your favorite authors will be visiting a city near you

- Search for and order backlist books from our online catalog

- Check out author bios and background information

- Send e-mail to your favorite authors

- Meet the Kensington staff online

- Join us in weekly chats with authors, readers and other guests

- Get writing guidelines

- AND MUCH MORE!

Visit our website at http://www.kensingtonbooks.com